POWER PLAY

BLADES HOCKEY NOVEL

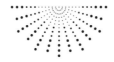

MARIA LUIS

ALKMINI BOOKS, LLC

He (was) the NHL's hottest goalie.
I (am) a struggling sports journalist on the verge of losing it all.

My stick-in-the-mud boss is determined to make my life hell. He sits in my office and lays down an ultimatum: get an exclusive interview with the NHL's golden boy, Duke Harrison, or I'll be out on my a*s.

No *way* am I letting my future rest on the broad shoulders of a goalie who's three seasons past his prime.

I've got eight days to convince Duke that the loyal fans of *The Cambridge Tribune* (annual circulation: 1,000) are dying to know about his life, on and off the ice. Eight days to face off against the sexy man who's hellbent on blocking my shot at every turn.

This power play is going to be one for the pucking ages.

Published by Alkmini Books, LLC.

Cover design by Najla Qamber Designs

Editing by Jackety.

❀ Created with Vellum

Boston, I may hate your snow, but I will always miss your aggressive driving, Dunkin' Donuts, and your passion for all things sports.

And to you, Mama - may we live our dreams to the fullest and enjoy life each and every day.

Good job, honey.

PROLOGUE

BOSTON, MASSACHUSETTS

PRESENT DAY

*D*uke's fingers slip the length of my silk dress up my calves, exposing my skin to the chilly night air. His hands are strong, powerful . . . deliciously warm. The glittering cityscape fades behind the breadth of his shoulders, and I'm left with the shocking realization that . . .

Oh, my god, this is happening.

Me. Duke Harrison. The promise of intimacy in a place that isn't intimate at all.

I should probably fill you in on a secret: I like sex.

I know what you're thinking: "Charlie, why in the hell do I need to know what action your lady parts have or have not received? Get back to the sexy times with that Duke guy!"

There's a catch, though. While I might *like* sex, that doesn't mean I'm all that good at it. The last time I had the (mis)fortune of getting down and dirty with a guy, he informed me that I was a frigid Ice Queen. Mid-sexy times. (Because *that's* romantic).

Now, the Ice Queen thing, I get that often. Not sweat off my back.

But the *frigid* part, that was offensive. I wasn't being frigid; I just didn't think his *jab-jab-jab* finger technique was up to par. Okay, I *may* have asked him to ease up a little, because I'm not the sort of woman who just silently takes it till the cows come home. It's not my fault that he got all high-and-mighty and blamed me for wasting his time.

Not. My. Fault.

It's called having standards.

Until Duke. If he were to demand, "Panties off, now," you can bet your derrière that my Target-grade underwear would hit the floor faster than my favorite Dunkin' Donuts barista makes my iced coffee every morning.

To the regular Average Joe strolling down Boston's Commonwealth Avenue, my panties wouldn't leave my hips. But this is Duke Harrison we're talking about, and I'm currently making out with him on the rooftop of the Omni Parker House, Boston's fanciest hotel, like we're nothing more than a horny pair of teenagers. God bless our souls.

That's what happens when the guy you've been lusting after puts his hand between your legs and whispers your name in a husky voice made from silk and unicorns. You lose all mental capacity to think straight.

Although, if we're being all honest here, I haven't really been thinking straight since I first met him.

CHAPTER ONE

ONE WEEK EARLIER . . .

I'm late.

As in, I'm hobbling on one foot in my 600-square foot apartment, trying to yank on my favorite pair of knee-high boots, even as I foam at the mouth courtesy of the toothbrush sticking out of it.

Multi-tasking at its finest, really.

"Charlie, we are going to be *late*," my best friend says from her perch on my couch. Jenny Halverton has never been late in her entire life, and I can say this with a good deal of confidence, as we've been best friends since the second grade. She weirdly thrives on being the first to arrive, whether it's for prom (do you know how weird it is to be the first group to show up?), her college graduation (also weird), and her wedding (understandable, except for the fact that she beat the groom by about thirty minutes, which, once again, made it weird for the rest of us).

"I'm hurrying," I slur around my purple Oral-B toothbrush. My booted foot lands on the hardwood floor with an echoing *thud*.

My third-floor apartment is small, and I swear the ancient glass-paned windows shake in their tracks when I hook up my other foot and let it land with the same level of force.

As a former hockey player, I'm not the most delicate of creatures, though I've certainly spent the last few years attempting to slim down my muscular frame and act a little more feminine.

I've succeeded for the most part, aside for my tree-trunk thighs. I've accepted that we are now life-long partners, for better or for worse.

Jenny eyes me with barely-concealed disgust when I spit in the kitchen and leave my toothbrush to conduct a balancing act on the lip of the sink. "What?" I snag my coat from where I tossed it over the Formica bar earlier. "You said that we're in a hurry."

"It would have taken you an extra five seconds to do that in the bathroom." Her dark gaze pointedly flicks toward my shoebox of a restroom. "Five seconds," she repeats for effect.

Rolling my blue eyes to the ceiling, I counter, "It's taken you five seconds to reprimand me, *Mom*. Shouldn't we be leaving?"

Jenny concedes with a theatrical sigh, and I grin as I grab my car keys from the entryway table. It's not my fault that she's a stickler for certain things: timeliness, cleanliness, and a whole lot of other words that end with –iness suffixes that I can't bother to think of right now.

We take the stairs—no elevator in my Cambridge triple-decker—and make our way to my car. It's a cute, white Prius, a twenty-sixth birthday present to myself from a few months ago. I say this as though I regularly buy myself expensive gifts.

Not true.

My last car was fifteen years old and counting, a total death trap, and to get it to start I had to spend five to seven minutes shoving a butter knife into its gear shift as I whispered sweet nothings against the steering wheel.

We parted quite amicably after she died and left me stranded on the side of the road in Middle-of-Nowhere, western Massachusetts.

I slide into my new baby, patting the dashboard with a happy sigh, and tap the start button to the left of the wheel. The engine hums to life on cue.

God, life is good sometimes.

"We're not that late," I tell Jenny as we turn off my street. A car honks behind me when I cut it off, but this is Boston, and I am nothing less than the driver my dad taught me to be: aggressively dickish. "In fact," I add, "some might say that we're *early*."

Jenny grumbles into her thick, floral scarf. "We're late."

"Girl, we aren't Mel's maids of honor. We don't actually have to show up an hour early to this thing."

We're on our way to our friend's bachelorette party, though the wedding isn't taking place for another month. We met Mel during our sophomore year at Boston University, and have been thick as thieves ever since. Alas, Mel is one of six sisters, leaving Jenny and I to serve as mere guests at her wedding.

This upsets Jenny way more than it ever bothered me. Despite having a more subdued personality, Jenny strangely lives for the moments when she becomes the center of attention.

I, on the other hand, live for the moments when I can hug a wall and pretend I'm wearing my PJs and reading a book. When Mel informed me that she didn't have room for me in her bridal party, it took everything in my power to not fist pump the air.

Thankfully, my responsibilities now languish among the Just Show Up variety.

Knowing that Jenny is wallowing in self-imposed guilt over our "tardiness," I bring up a topic that I know will infuse the color back into her cheeks. "Do you think Gwen will be there today?"

Jenny gives a little growl. "I hope not."

I bang a U-ey and head for Harvard Square, where TeaLicious (the start of our day) is located. "Still feeling sour about it?"

"She flirted with my *husband*. Of course I'm sour about it."

Mel's cousin, Gwen, is nothing if not classy.

"Ty put her in her place, though. Hell, one more second and I really thought he would Heisman her."

There's another growl from Jenny in the passenger's seat. "First," she says, holding up a finger, "No more sports analogies outside of work. We've talked about this. Second"— another finger goes up—"I know that Ty would *never* cheat on me, especially not with that . . . "

Jenny trails off and I help her out. "Evil witch? Crazy nut-job? Home-wrecker? Let me know when I've reached the magnitude of your hatred for her."

"We'll be here all day," she sniffs, and I can't help but laugh because it's true.

Over the years, I've been forced to hang out with Mel's cousin frequently enough. At first I didn't mind so much. We were in college and she's one of those girls who possesses so much confidence that you can't help but hope just a little bit of it will superglue itself to you. Permanently.

For a girl like me—a former hockey player and a young lady with no skill for flirtation—Gwen was like a shiny, redheaded beacon of inspiration.

It wasn't so much that I liked her, but rather, I wanted to emulate her feminine confidence, a feminine confidence which I myself lacked in droves.

Sleek hair? Well, there wasn't much that I could do to my kinky blonde hair, but I certainly did my best with the inexpensive flat iron I purchased from the convenient store.

Leafy greens for breakfast, lunch, and dinner? I lasted only two weeks before realizing that my extreme level of activity demanded a high-protein diet, and *no,* I could not subsist on spinach and cottage cheese for every meal.

Glamorous make up? My winged liner looked a bit savage, but if I tilted my head *just right* both my right and left eyes looked even enough, I suppose.

It took all of three weeks for me to realize that Gwen existed on an unachievable ethereal plane. Subsequently allowing me to see that . . . Well, she wasn't all that kind. A five-letter word that rhymes with "itch" would be a more appropriate description of Gwen James.

"I heard through the grapevine that she's seeing someone now," I tell Jenny as I pull my car into the TeaLicious parking lot. It's packed to the brim, and I beeline for the remaining empty spot. "Ty's sensibilities will now be safe."

"Thank God."

We laugh at the same time and then climb out of my Prius.

TeaLicious is by far one of the most hipster-populated places I've ever visited. Think wine bar but with tea instead. It also happens to be Mel's favorite place in the Boston-metro area, and therefore it only made sense to kick off her last few weeks of Singledom by drinking one too many cups of Earl Grey.

What can I say? Some people prefer rum and coke; Mel James prefers orange-scented tea that spent a former lifetime as a jolly-rancher.

We give the party name to the hostess and she's quick to point us in the direction of the group of shrieking women at the back of the restaurant.

I purposely avoid making eye contact with Jenny as we sidle up to the group.

Mel spots us almost immediately, and she launches up from her chair to book it straight over, her arms outstretched. "You're *here!*" she cries, cupping my face in her hands as she plants a smacking kiss on each of my cheeks. She does the same to Jenny, who squirms at the too-close contact.

Whereas Jenny carries hand-sanitizer everywhere she goes, Mel James—soon to be Mel Wellers—has no idea that some people require personal space.

"Charlie was running late again," Jenny drawls, effectively throwing me under the bus.

I huff a little at that, even though it is sort of true. To Mel, I say, "I accidentally slept through my alarm. I didn't go to bed until late last night."

"Hot date?" Mel asks with a dash of hope in her expression.

I hate to disappoint her, seeing as how *my* love life is as silent as a graveyard, but . . .

"No, I was at work. You'd think that the boss man would want to head home early on a Friday night. Not the case. He decided at six p.m. on the dot that he wanted me to do research for a feature piece on Duke Harrison's shit-tastic game from Thursday."

Mel's right eye twitches in that way it does when she's hiding something. I pause, waiting for her to speak up like she always does when something is eating away at her.

She doesn't, so I add, "I don't get why everyone's obsessed with Harrison. I mean, all right, he plays for the NHL. He's quick with his hands, and he's relatively good-looking—if you like that my-teeth-might-not-be-my-own appeal, which isn't really my thing."

"Sounds like someone's got a crush," Jenny snickers from beside me, and I promptly shoot her the bird. She mimes catching it, then ignites my offering in a pit of imaginary fire. Lovely.

"I don't have a crush," I mutter, tucking my crazy blonde hair behind one ear. You can dress me in fine clothes, but my hair is a beast of its own. There's no taming it. "All I'm saying," I stress slowly, "is that he should have retired by now. Just because he was a hotshot goalie for the last decade doesn't mean that he's adept at protecting the net anymore. He's weak."

"Thank you."

I flinch at the masculine voice behind me, my gaze immediately seeking help from my two best friends. Both Mel and Jenny look up at the ceiling, and I instantly kick them off of my short-but-sweet best friends list.

You see, there's the minute fact that I recognize that voice. I spent *six goddamn hours* listening to interviews on YouTube last night, and that husky baritone was featured in every single video I clicked.

I *really* don't want to turn around and face the music, and I can practically hear my bones creak in protest as I do so. My thoughts go something like this:

Ah, shit.

Why is this happening to me?

What Karma did I accrue?

And, most importantly, *what the* hell *is Duke Harrison of the Boston Blades doing here?*

When I turn around, I have my answer.

Mel's cousin Gwen is suctioned to Duke Harrison's side like an octopus after its next meal. I'm not kidding. Her arm is wrapped around his back, her fingers stuffed into the front pocket of his jeans. Her bottle-dyed red hair cascades over his arm, she's that close to him. Unsurprisingly, she's shooting daggers at me with her eyes.

I blink back at her coolly, just to show that I won't be bullied.

Then I take my first look at Duke Harrison in the flesh and I'm surprised to find that I'm still standing.

I blink rapidly in an attempt to refresh my vision. My first glimpse of him has to be faulty, because there's no way that he is as hot as—

Holy baby Jesus. The camera does him no justice, no justice at all. He's huge, which is to be expected of a professional athlete of his caliber. Broad shoulders, encased in a black, fitted button-down shirt, taper into a fit waist. His jaw is cut from granite, which I understand makes no sense at all, but that doesn't even matter. A cleft punctures his chin. Honestly, I'm shocked by the handsomeness of his rugged features, not to mention his thick head of golden hair.

His overall attractiveness is almost unfair.

Blue eyes, the color of a bird's egg, narrow down at me. I ignore the obvious annoyance in his expression to continue my slow once-over of Boston's Hottest Bachelor Under 40.

Except, by the looks of things, he's not a bachelor any longer.

An engagement ring glitters on Gwen's left hand. It's huge. Probably the size of a toy poodle. If she punched someone with that thing, they'd be laid out cold in a heartbeat.

I inch back, just in case she gets any ideas. Gwen and *ideas* aren't commonly associated with one another, but you never really know. Once, when we were all in college, Gwen snatched a woman's hair at a club and ripped out a handful after the girl told Gwen that her dress was hideous.

I may not particularly like my hair—doesn't mean that I want to have any bald spots on my scalp.

"Charlie," Gwen says now, her voice a pitch lower than Death's. "This is Duke Harrison."

Mel makes a choking noise behind me. I feel no remorse. Serves her right for not alerting me to the fact that *Duke freakin' Harrison* has been standing right behind me this whole time.

I force a smile, hoping that my red lipstick hasn't imprinted on my teeth from all of my recent gnashing, and blandly murmur, "How lovely."

I look up, up, up to Duke's face. I'm not exactly petite, but nor is he exactly average in height. Towering over me, he must be at least six-foot-something. He's still watching me, I notice, his full mouth twisted in a frown. It's sort of sexy now that I'm up close. His face, I mean, not the frown. Although the frown isn't too bad either. It's sulky, a little brooding. I find that I like it.

Gwen glowers and I realize that my greeting hasn't met her standard. For the sake of not throwing down at my best friend's bachelorette party, I try again. "It's so lovely to meet you, Duke. What made you decide to join our women-only tea party?"

Jenny joins the fake-choking train. My lips finally tug upward in a genuine smile.

Duke Harrison, goalie extraordinaire for the Boston Blades, does not return my smile. "Gwen encouraged me to come," is all he says.

"Ah."

It's all that needs to be said, really. What Gwen wants she generally gets—aside from Jenny's husband, that is. My gaze flicks down to Gwen's hand and the diamond ring sparkling under the soft, overhead lighting. "Maybe she wants you in the wedding planning mood," I say. "You know, to bring you up to snuff."

"We're not together."

Now I'm the one gasping for air. I pound my fist against my chest, rubbing in tight little circles. And, oh God, my eyes —they're stinging. Laughter, I think, not tears. Gwen's mouth opens and shuts, even as her gaze turns squinty.

"I was just *trying* it on my ring finger," she snaps. Yanking the diamond off her fourth finger, she fits it on her middle finger of the opposite hand. "Just to see how I feel about it. Duke likes to play hard to get."

"I'm not playing anything," he says evenly.

I can hear Gwen grinding her teeth from here. If she does so any harder, she'll turn them to dust. With her hand still wrapped around his arm, I nevertheless have the sneaking suspicion that while they might not be *together* they've probably swapped spit a few times. Crossed each other's hockey sticks, if you know what I mean—not that Gwen's got a penis. At least, I'm not aware of her having a penis.

Regardless, even if they *haven't* done the dirty, it's clear from the dog-in-heat expression on Gwen's face that she wants to get close and personal with Duke Harrison's twin pucks.

I glance over at Duke, expecting to see that same look of lust darkening his blue eyes. Instead, he appears bored. A little on edge, maybe, but there's no flare of desire in his expression when he attempts to pull away from Gwen's death grip.

Suddenly our gazes clash, hold, and I lift my brow, as if to say, *I wouldn't bother trying.*

He returns my brow-lift with one of his own, and I read his message loud and clear: *Get her off of me.*

My shoulders lift in a shrug—*not my problem*, it translates to—and I notice a pulse leap to his jaw.

"We have an event to go to after this," Gwen says, oblivious to the fact that the man beside her is on the verge of fleeing. "Duke agreed to be my date."

With a heavy sigh, Duke finally manages to detangle himself from the octopus otherwise known as Gwen James. "I'm not your date," he grumbles in overt frustration, "I'm your damn cl—"

Whatever he's about to say is cut off by Gwen's high-pitched voice: "It doesn't matter. *Tea*, Duke? Let's go grab some tea."

She doesn't wait to make any more small talk, not even with her bride-to-be cousin. Latching her hand around his wrist, she gives a quick tug and pulls him toward the table of women.

"Excuse me," Duke murmurs as he brushes past me. I objectively admire his butt as he walks away. It's a great butt, no doubt thanks to the fact that he's constantly squatting in the net. He moves like a lethal predator, and there's no shortage of female sighs as he settles into an empty chair at the end of the table. Gwen sits next to him, immediately turning to him with an accusing finger jab.

Trouble in paradise, it seems.

And then it hits me: I just met Duke "The Mountain" Harrison. *Holy crap*. This is . . . this is crazy. I cannot *wait* to tell Casey, my coworker, on Monday morning. Even if I do think he's overrated, there's still the fact that I am a sports journalist and I've been following his career for years. Since he was a rookie a decade ago.

But while I might be a sports journalist, I also happen to while away thirty-five hours per week at *The Cambridge Tribune*. To say that the newspaper is second-rate would be a stretch, and for one very good reason: my boss, Josh, doesn't believe in handing out press badges. No one takes us seriously because half of the city doesn't even know that we exist.

Who wants to read an online newspaper where the quotes are regurgitated from other publications? No one knows who I am—this isn't a bad thing, necessarily—but my chances of even freelancing for a more reputable newsletter, like *The Boston Globe*, are slim to none.

Honestly, *I* wouldn't even hire me.

My clips are decent, but there's only so much that you can do with lackluster story material.

"I don't like that look on your face," Jenny says from beside me. "Whatever you're thinking, you stop that right now, Charlie Denton."

Bristling at her suspicious tone, I say, "I'm not thinking about anything."

"You are," Mel jumps in. "You so are."

They've got my calling card. I need a story—a story that will land on screens all over the Northeast—and Duke Harrison just became my muse.

CHAPTER TWO

I wait until Monday to make my move.

I'm surprised I've contained my nervous energy for this long, actually. This is it—my opportunity to make it into the big leagues. I can feel it in my bones, though I'm hoping that the echoing pain in my shins isn't an early onset of arthritis kicking in.

"What's the matter with you?" my coworker demands after I leave my desk twice in the span of thirty minutes to pour myself more coffee.

Casey and I didn't start out as best buddies. In fact, it's safe to say that we spent our first year at *The Cambridge Tribune* hating each other's guts. Desperation, as well as the creeping realization that we had only each other in a department full of testosterone, soon bonded us in a way that could only be trumped by slicing our forearms and sharing our blood.

I dump a packet of creamer into my mug, swirling the coffee around with the bottom of a plastic fork. "I have this idea," I tell her as I sit back down in my lumpy office chair. "Do you want to hear it?"

Casey rolls her eyes but gestures for me to go on. Instinctively, I know this means she's agitated by my jitters but curious enough to keep quiet. We've been through this before.

"Okay." I plunk my mug down and coffee sloshes over the rim. Idly I use a spare paper napkin from yesterday's Dunkins run to wipe it up. "Guess who I met this weekend."

"Your future husband."

She says this so drolly that I glower. Is it so hard to imagine me as the marrying kind? I think of my previous track record and feel my shoulders slump in defeat.

"That was a joke," Casey tells me, making the defeat feel only that much sharper. "Obviously we're going to become two old cat ladies together."

"I don't like cats."

"This is why we can't be lesbians and marry," Casey jokes, pushing her brown hair back from her face. "I couldn't be with someone who hates God's greatest gift to mankind."

This time, it's my turn to roll my eyes. The marriage thing is a running joke between us, mainly because our coworkers are sexist pigs and have a hard time believing that, yes, both Casey and I are straight, and yes, we thoroughly enjoy sports.

I cut straight to the chase. "I met Duke Harrison."

Casey's eyes go wide and her mouth falls open a little. "I don't think I heard you correctly. Did you just say that you met *Duke Harrison*?"

I nod. "Yes. And, before you ask, he's only marginally better looking in person than he is on TV."

The doubtful expression she levels on me says it all. "*Only* marginally better looking?" she demands, dropping her elbows to her desk. "I refuse to believe that Duke Harrison is anything less than a Greek God."

Sipping my coffee, I offer a shrug and lie. "Sorry to disappoint."

16

She doesn't look like she believes me worth a damn, but we have bigger fish to fry.

Like how we're going to rope Duke Harrison into an exclusive interview with *The Cambrige Tribune*. I've been thinking about this nonstop for the last two days and my current plan is full of Swiss cheese grated holes. In theory, it's goddamn brilliant: Duke Harrison agrees to give a one-of-a-kind interview to *The Cambridge Tribune* and, in turn, Casey and I are taken seriously within our sphere of peers.

Maybe we get offers from *The Globe* or *The Herald* (ugh, I'm so not a fan of *The Boston Herald*). Maybe we don't. Maybe Duke Harrison laughs in my face and has his security team wheel me out on a stretcher as a mentally unstable patient.

Is moving up my career worth the price of possibly going to jail?

No.

Maybe.

Probably, yes.

I fill Casey in on my plan, choosing my words carefully. When I finish, she leans back in her equally lumpy chair and steeples her fingers, elbows planted on the chair's armrests. Nervously, my knee bounces up and down, and I press my hand flat against my thigh to keep it still.

"What do you think?"

She watches me from behind thick-wired frames. It's the same expression my mom used to give me just before she embarked on an hour-long lecture. Instinctively, I gird myself for the worst.

"I think . . . "

My eyes slam shut.

"I think it's brilliant! How do we get this done?"

A sigh of relief escapes me. Okay. Okay, this is good. I take a deep breath to steady my nerves. *Think of the job,*

Charlie. Yes, the job. My gaze sweeps over our shared office. It's a sad-looking time transport to 1976. The only thing missing is a shaggy rug the color of stale Cheetos.

The time has come to take big steps.

I've thought about this all morning. Gwen knows him. In theory, I could reach out to her and ask for Duke's contact information, but something tells me that she'd bury me six feet under before she ever helped a girl out. "I need his email address," I announce.

Casey rolls her eyes. "Oh, you *only* need his email address." She sticks a pen in her mouth and bites down on the cap. "There is no way we're going to be able to find his email. Maybe an email for his PR agent, sure, but his personal one?" She shakes her head. "You're out of your mind."

I knew she'd say that. I down the rest of my coffee, then forlornly glance down into my trash bin at the empty Dunkin' Donuts Styrofoam cup from this morning. The crappy work stuff will just have to do for now.

"The PR email is blocked," I tell Casey. "You know, one of those websites where they want a subscription in exchange for your soul? Nothing on the guy's official website either, which is a bit surprising."

She blinks. "He has an official website?"

"Yes."

"Show me."

My eyes narrow. "There's nothing exciting on there. Stats, a few pictures—that sort of thing. I did fill out the contact form, but we all know how those work out. I'll never hear back from—"

"Is he shirtless in any of the photos?"

"What?" Now it's my turn to blink. "It's not PornHub, Casey."

A blush stains her cheeks, and she busies herself with

sorting a stack of papers on her desk. "I didn't ask if he was *naked*, just if he didn't have a shirt on."

I stare at her. "You're sick, you know that?"

"No, I'm a woman with hormones and Duke Harrison is one fine male specimen."

Rolling my eyes, I turn back to my desk. I need to figure this out. From what I've gathered, Duke "The Mountain" is a private enough guy. I type his name into Google because, what the hell, *no one* can escape Google's web crawler, and I specifically remember bypassing a Twitter page during my research on him last week.

And I'm right—up pops his official Twitter profile. I can work with this. I tap the mouse on the appropriate link, and wait for the little circle of death to do its thing and then I'm in.

His profile photo is one of him posing for a 'Got Milk' ad. Truth be told, I didn't even think they made those commercials anymore. But there he is in all of his glory.

Shirtless.

Mouth-wateringly bare-chested with hard abs for days.

I quickly glance at Casey, but she's so absorbed in her game of solitaire that I give in to temptation and enlarge the photo.

Eight.

That's the number of tight ridges he's got on his washboard stomach. Maybe *I'm* the one who's sick.

I squirm a little in my chair and read his profile. It's short and overtly direct:

NHL Goalie – Boston Blades.
Seasons: Not Enough.

Not so chatty of an individual, is he? If he had an online

dating profile, I imagine it would read something like, "I like it hot & dirty in the sheets. No repeats."

Whereas if *I* had a dating profile, it would go a little something like this: "Looking for long-term relationship. Likes dogs, Thai food, and needs a boyfriend who doesn't mind it when girlfriend chooses to watch the Patriots over engaging in sexy-times."

Now that I think about it, I may have discovered the reason for my constant singleness.

"Casey," I say, distracting myself from Duke's naked chest on the computer screen, "if you had one chance to tweet at a hockey player and capture his attention, what would you say?"

"Am I trying to get laid?" she asks. She spins her chair around to face me, and I hastily exit out of Duke Harrison's Twitter page before she can see that I've been ogling his beautiful body.

"What?" I exclaim. "No. You're trying to get a *story* out of him."

Her head tilts to the side. "Be honest. Just ask him for the interview."

Yeah, I could have figured that one out myself. Flexing my fingers, I turn to my computer and go for broke. At the end of the day, what's the worst that could happen?

CHAPTER THREE

N^{o.} I wake up the next morning to find that two-letter word in my Twitter DM inbox.

No. Just like that.

I suppose I should feel grateful that Duke bothered replying to my clumsy tweet, not to mention he took the time to follow me in order to, you know, slide into my DMs.

Except that I'm not grateful. In fact, I'm annoyed. He may be a professional hockey player, but I'm one step away from being a no-name journalist for the rest of my life. I need something big.

I need an interview with Duke Harrison.

Clambering out of bed, I drag my body into the kitchen and turn on the coffee machine. Then, I sit my butt down on my bar stool and stare at the message again for the umpteenth time this morning.

No.

It would be so easy to accept defeat. To slink back to *The Tribune*'s office and wallow in my self-pity as I quote other journalists with far more expansive pedigrees for the rest of my life.

Or . . . I can take a risk.

I pull my phone toward me. Stare down at it. And then, before allowing myself to rethink my decision, I begin to type. I hit send.

I'm not sure if you remember me. I met you the other day at TeaLicious for the bachelorette party?

The coffee beeps its timely arrival and I pour myself a mug of the hot brew. I'll need a stop by Dunkins' on the way to work this morning if I ever want to function like a normal human being. It's part of my regular routine. A routine I love. If only I could bring my career up to par.

As if working on similar brainwaves, my phone chimes with an incoming message and I launch myself at it.

"Breathe, Charlie," I order myself, "breathe."

He's responded.

Thank you, Jesus.

Cautiously, I tap in my cell phone's password, flick my finger to the right to bring up the Twitter page and—

I remember you. The answer is still no.

What. The. Hell.

I gulp down some coffee, only to belatedly realize that it is *scalding hot.* "Crap!" I shout at my empty apartment, pressing my tongue to the roof of my mouth to soothe the sudden throbbing.

And then I'm back at my cell phone because what type of answer is that? Is he even capable of writing complex sentences?

It's a syntax travesty, I tell you.

May I ask why not? I tap out. Hit send. Make a silent prayer to the hockey gods to be on my side today.

His answer arrives in seconds. **No.**

My teeth clench. *Is it because I called you overrated?*

Thanks for the reminder. Now the answer is definitely a no.

The deepening urge to hurl my phone across the room has me actually going so far as to lift my arm and aim for the window.

"Get a hold of yourself," I mutter. "You're a professional journalist."

That's right. I may work for a dead-beat publication with a circulation of perhaps 1,000—per *year*—but that doesn't mean I don't hold any leverage in this situation. I stare at the last message he's sent me. I type something out and then delete it.

Ultimately, I go for the pathetic route. *Five questions. You can answer here on Twitter.*

Not interested.

Three questions. I'll throw in dinner.

Realizing that he could interpret that as an invitation for a date, I quickly send off another message: *What I mean is, I'll give you a gift card for dinner. Dinner does not include me.*

My cheeks heat at the flirtatious undertone, but it's too late to retract the words now. I quickly glance at the clock above the stove. I need to get ready for work. Only, I'm glued to my barstool.

Glued to the possibility that Duke Harrison might answer me back.

He does, and I can practically hear his husky baritone reverberate through the words. **That's too bad. Dinner with you sounds more interesting . . .**

I wait impatiently.

More interesting than . . . *what?* More interesting than conducting an interview? More interesting than undergoing a prostrate exam? There are endless possibilities, and I'm dying to know exactly what he means by that cryptic message.

Before I even have the chance to formulate a response, I receive another message: **But the answer to your request is still no. Have a good day, Charlie.**

Damn it.

I drain the rest of my now lukewarm coffee and stand up. This isn't over. As I start pulling my clothes off to take a shower, I call Casey. I don't care that it's seven in the morning. This is important. Plus, she's called me at this time of day more than once when I've had to pick her up from a one-night-stand's house.

In comparison, my phone call is tame.

She answers on the third ring, her voice raspy with sleep. "What do you want, woman?"

"He said no." I turn the shower on and stare at myself in the mirror as the water heats up. I look crazy. My already curly hair is turning more voluminous with the steam from the shower, and my blue eyes are dark with anticipation. On the ice, my teammates often called me "Crazy Charlie" because of my impulsiveness in the sport.

I was methodical to a point. Then, impulse drove me, both on the ice and off.

"Who said no?" Casey asks. Her voice sounds muffled, like she's driven her face into her pillow in an effort to ignore me.

"Duke Harrison. He DM'ed me on Twitter."

"Are you really that surprised?"

"Well, no. But that doesn't mean that this can't actually happen. We can get this interview."

"You mean that *you* can get this interview. I'm flying on your coattails, girl."

It frustrates me, just slightly, when Casey says stuff like this. I recognize that I'm ambitious, sometimes to a fault, but it often feels like I'm the only who gives a damn at *The Tribune*.

I shake off the Negative Nancy vibes, swiping a palm over the mirror as it begins to fog up. "I need Gwen. She was with him the other day."

"Don't we hate her?"

"Yes," I say with a shrug that she can't see. "There's no way around it. I could reach out through the contact form again but what would that do? My email would end up in the trash folder and he's already told me no personally."

She heaves a great, beleaguered sigh. "Maybe you should take this as a sign that he doesn't actually *want* to do the interview?"

I toe off my fuzzy slippers. "I know that he doesn't want to."

"Then why are we still pursuing this?"

Sticking my hand into the shower, I test the temperature. Lukewarm, as per usual. My apartment isn't exactly fitted with the latest indoor plumbing. I'm just grateful that the previous property owners tore out the original shared bathroom in the hallway from the 1930s, and installed personal ones in each apartment.

"Because, Casey," I say firmly, "this is what real journalists do. They chase down their leads. They get it done."

"There's a difference between journalists and tabloid reporters. One does a lot more stalking."

"I'm not stalking the man." He's more attractive than I originally thought, yes, but I'm not one to set myself up for failure on a romantic level.

Going for a guy like Duke Harrison would be the worst decision I could ever make in my life.

"I'm calling for a double date," I finally say. "Think about it. Gwen's clearly wanting to date the guy. He, on the other hand, seems to want anything but that. It's a dirty move, I know, but I think that I can swing it. Gwen would never pass up the opportunity to lord it over me that her date is a professional hockey player. Subtlety is not in her biology. "

"Some would say it's not in yours either," Casey injects wryly, and the foggy mirror reflects my pained grimace.

"This could be a game-changer, Casey. This time next year we could be sitting in a fantabulous office at *The Globe,* and laughing over all the miserable time we've spent holed up where we are now."

We fall silent and I imagine that we are both thinking of our office at *The Tribune.* It's a wreck. The paint is peeling on the walls, and there is an unidentifiable red stain on the carpet that has been there since I was hired three years ago. I don't know what it is, but my sneaking suspicion is that someone committed murder in there and we're all under surveillance.

Just a theory, of course.

Casey draws my attention back to our conversation when she says, "Okay, matter of importance. Who're you going to ask to be your date?"

I hold my gaze in the mirror. And then, in the most serious voice I can manage, I say, "Your twin."

CHAPTER FOUR

*C*asey's twin, Caleb, squeals when I pull up outside of his apartment building. I should be embarrassed that I have no other dating prospects than a man who bats for the other team, but Caleb is honestly one of the sweetest people I know. Plus, he's aware of the Plan.

Step One: Go on a date with Gwen and Duke.

Step Two: Somehow lure Duke into private conversation, in which I propose that he give me an interview for *The Tribune*.

Step Three: Gain recognition as a successful sports journalist.

Step Four: I have no Step Four. I deliberated about it in the shower this morning and, honestly, I'd be ecstatic just to *interview* the guy. Even if he has been sucking on the ice in recent seasons, and even if I do think he should promptly retire.

I somehow convinced my boss to let the feature on Duke slide, as I told him that I had plans for something better. He didn't ask me what those plans were. I'm half-terrified that I'm about to get the can.

"Get in, get in," I tell Caleb, unlocking the passenger's side door so he can jump in.

When he sees me, he gives a little howl of pleasure. "You look delectable," he says enthusiastically. "That dress? Where did you get it?"

"Target." I edge my car across two lanes, bypassing at least three angry drivers who honk their horns and visibly roll down their windows to shout obscenities at me. "In the sales section."

"Really?" Caleb peers closer like he doesn't believe me. "How much?"

"Eleven dollars. I'm on a budget."

The Cambridge Tribune doesn't exactly pay well. In the past, I've picked up freelancing gigs on the side, using them to balance out my income into something a little more substantial. Lately, however, there just hasn't been enough time. I think Josh is feeling the pressure of subscriptions dropping and local advertisers pulling out, and Casey and I have had to pick up extra hours creating ads with absolutely no graphic design background.

I would say that it's been a fun experience, but that would be a bald-faced lie.

"Hmm," Caleb murmurs. He runs a hand through his neatly trimmed brown hair. "Very nice. If I were straight, I'd tap that."

"If you were straight," I say with a laugh, "you'd be tapping someone much better looking than me." With a free hand, I tug at the hem of the dress, which has inched up my thighs. "Okay. Let's go over this again. Gwen is who?"

"The evil witch of the west," he deadpans. "Girl, we'll be fine. Unless she actually starts melting in front of me, there's nothing to worry about."

Actually, there is *everything* to worry about. What if Duke Harrison sees straight through me? What if he takes one look at me and turns the other way? What if Gwen attempts to slaughter me at the table, à la *Game of Thrones'* Red Wedding? These are all probable outcomes, and my brain has been stuck on repeat for two days now, overthinking every last one of them.

By the time we roll up to the restaurant, we're right on time. My nerves turn my palms into shallow pools of sweat and I carelessly run them down the length of my new dress. I spare a quick glance downward. I suppose the red sheath number *is* pretty. In an understated, simple sort of way.

We give the host our name and then wait off to the side for the other half of our party. I turn to Caleb, panic lining my voice when I ask, "What if they don't show?"

Caleb plucks my hand off his arm and gives it a quick squeeze. "We eat, drink champagne, and go home to our separate beds. It'll be the best date we've both ever had."

He may be kidding about himself, but his assumption is still relatively accurate on my end. I don't recall the last time I had a proper date. If I can't remember, then it has obviously been way too long.

Glancing down at my wristwatch, I check the time. They're late. By a minute. Jenny would be climbing up a wall right now. I settle my nerves by imagining my future desk at *The Boston Globe*. This will work. I just need a little faith, that's all.

"Oh, my God, don't you just look so *precious,* Charlie!"

I'm struck by both the relief that we haven't been stood up by the power couple, as well as a heavy dose of annoyance that Gwen has made me feel like a toddler trying on my mother's clothes.

I twist around, forcing a strained smile to my face. My smile falters a little when I catch sight of Gwen. She is also wearing a red dress, though hers is at least two times more revealing. The front cuts down between her breasts and the hem cuts short just below her crotch. I can't help but wonder if she's cold. I'd be cold; my crotch would be cold. It's thirty degrees outside and the weather forecast this morning called for flurries.

She's either stupidly brave or asking for a case of strep throat.

Possibly both.

She holds out her hands, gathering me in for a hug like a long-lost friend. I'm not fooled in the slightest, and gingerly pull back from the witch's claws. "It's good to see you," I say, looking from Gwen to Duke.

He stares back at me. His blue gaze is furious, and I busy myself with drawing Caleb forward and making introductions.

Stick to the plan.

Suddenly I'm wondering if this was a good idea.

The host sidles up to us, his mouth dropping open a little at the sight of Duke. He recovers admirably. "Would you all come this way?" he says, his voice hovering just short of all-out awe. He lasts all of thirty seconds on the way to the table before he breaks. "Mr. Harrison, you're, like, my hero."

A grin tugs at the corner of Duke's mouth, and suddenly I know. I know what it is about him that makes women pant at the sight of him. It's utterly ridiculous, and I throw a can-you-believe-this look at Caleb only to realize that he too looks awestruck. Damn it.

Undaunted, Duke grins like he's totally accustomed to being fawned over by random strangers. "You a hockey fan?"

The host nods like a bobble-head doll. "Oh, man, yeah. When you made that final save against the Penguins a few weeks ago? It was fuck—I mean, it was fantastic."

Duke gives a low, husky laugh. I think Caleb just got a hard-on. I can't be certain, but he's walking funnily beside me now, and he keeps muttering "not now" to himself in a way that's increasingly suspicious. He's not alone. The host is blushing like an adolescent, and there's no doubt in my mind he's on the verge of asking for a selfie with the Blades' first round goalie.

"What's your name?"

In the face of Duke's question, the host halts in his tracks. "Um, Steve, Mr. Harrison. Steve Zet."

"All right, Steve Zet, you've got two tickets on me. Next game, just let the ticket booth know and they'll let you in."

Duke Harrison has just earned himself a life long fan, if the expression on Steve's face is anything to go by. Pure love. I've always wondered what it looks like and now I know.

It can easily be confused with constipation, so you have to look closely to distinguish the difference.

Steve finally seats us at our table, and a small game of who-gets-what-chair ensues. Gwen claims the seat closest to the crackling fireplace—I *knew* that she had to be cold—and then points a finger at Duke when he goes to sit next to her.

"No, no, not *there*. You can't sit there."

Duke looks toward Caleb and I. Hell if I know what her problem is. With a shrug, I take the seat diagonal to Gwen and plant my butt down. My feet are already on fire. You can put me in a nice dress but you can't make my feet accept the death traps that are better known as stilettos.

Gwen motions to the chair on my right. "There," she tells Duke, "sit across from me."

Caleb, bless his soul, is never one to let a snarky opportunity pass, and quips, "Gwen, if I start playing footsie with you, I apologize in advance. I'm just so accustomed to sitting *next* to my lovely Charlie that, well"—he shrugs boyishly —"it's a habit now. You've been forewarned." Then he pulls out his chair, plops down, and promptly plucks my hand off the table to kiss my knuckles.

He's laying it on thick. My nose scrunches as I ease my

fingers out of his grip and go for my short glass of ice water. I barely manage a sip before the chair beside me screeches across the hardwood floor and Duke Harrison lowers his big body down onto it.

Almost immediately I'm assaulted by the scent of man, pine, and sexiness. Yes, sexiness has a scent. I've only *just* discovered it, seeing as how Duke just showed me that it existed, and I resist the urge to inch my chair to the right. I want to decipher what it is exactly that makes him smell so good.

As if knowing that I'm thinking insane thoughts, he tosses me a *stop-being-weird* look before slouching back in his chair. His crisp, blue button-down parts at the neck, revealing a tan throat and a hint of black ink.

He's tattooed. On his chest. Obviously his 'Got Milk' campaign is not from a recent photo shoot. I can't help but wonder if his rock hard stomach looks the same now as it did in that photo, whenever it was taken.

The stalker in me itches to snatch my phone from my purse and Google him again for a more recent shirtless photo. *What* is it that he has tattooed on his body? The question eats at me almost religiously. The mentally sane woman in me—the woman with a Plan—has no intention of Googling anyone. In fact, the sane part of me isn't even *interested* in him. For the following reasons:

1) He's obviously got something going on with Gwen James.

2) He's not my type.

3) He hates my guts, as evidenced by the fact that he keeps sending me dirty glances.

I'm back in control of my raging hormones by the time the server comes around for a drink order. Gwen opts for Dom Perignon—clearly, she's not expecting to pick up the tab tonight; Caleb chooses some sort of imported ale, and Duke goes for an American beer.

Sam Adams, a Boston classic.

"And you, Miss?" the server asks me politely.

"House white," I answer primly. If this bill is getting split into thirds, there's no way that I can afford much more than the outrageous entrée prices. My Target dress and I should have been left on the curb to rethink our life decisions.

Beside me, Duke shifts in his chair and his arm brushes up against mine. "Sorry," he says in a low voice, "I think these chairs were designed for someone . . . smaller."

It's the first time he's voluntarily spoken to me, as I'm not counting our Twitter private messages. Picking my words carefully, I say, "You are rather monstrous."

His face breaks into a half smile, but even that slight tilt to his lips warms his rugged looks. "Monstrous." He says the word with a shake of his head. "That's a new one."

From across the table, Caleb pipes up, "How tall *are* you?"

"Six-four," Gwen interjects. She throws a sickeningly sweet glance across the table at the man who has once again retreated into silence. "I know how much he weighs too."

I cough awkwardly into a closed fist at the same time that Caleb mouths "weirdo" before slamming back his ice water like it's straight Patron. If Gwen contents herself with making creepy comments all day, it's no wonder that Duke Harrison is practically a mute in her presence.

Why bother opening your mouth when you have a talking parrot to do the job for you?

In an attempt to smooth over the awkwardness which has taken hold of the table, I murmur, "That was real nice of you. With the host, I mean."

Duke passes a hand over his dark blond hair like the praise makes him uncomfortable. "It's nothing, really. I meet a lot of fans. A few tickets here and there isn't gonna hurt me."

"Duke is great with charity." This from Gwen, naturally.

I'm beginning to wonder if her mere existence is comprised of telling Duke Harrison what to do and alternatively acting as his pseudo-PR agent.

The server arrives with our drinks, takes our food order —I go for steak—and whisks away again, leaving the four of us to a miserable silence that I'm responsible for. The aura of fury radiating off Duke in waves has lessened, not that this does anything to ease the awkward vibe at the table. I swirl my white wine in its glass. Kick my foot out to Caleb. He kicks me back, and I withhold a taunt curse.

Surprisingly, it's Duke who breaks the pitiful reign of silence. "So, Caleb, what do you do for work?"

On cue, Caleb's shoulders inch back and he sits up straighter. "Oh, you *know*, this and that. Nothing as important as being a hockey player."

"He's a real estate agent," I tell Duke from the corner of my mouth, effectively killing Caleb's parade of mystery. "He wrangles in clients, promises them their HGTV dreams, and then takes their money."

Caleb's brows knit together. "You make me sound like a marauding pirate."

"Orlando Bloom or Johnny Depp?" I ask, and Duke once again surprises me by taking the question seriously.

His blue eyes focus on my fake-date, then slowly drags his gaze back to me. "Johnny Depp," Duke drawls, and it's as if he *knows* that his answer will light a fire under Caleb's butt because there's an unholy glimmer in his blue eyes. And, oh Lord, he's grinning now.

Widely.

At me.

"The left incisor is fake."

I jolt, feeling very much like I've stepped into a bucket of water, and then stuck my finger in an electrical socket, just for kicks. "What?"

Duke runs his tongue across his top left teeth. It's one of the hottest things I've ever seen. That one swipe of his tongue makes me feel dirty. I just took a shower, but I need another one immediately. Then, he reaches out to tap his left incisor. "This one," he says, "it's not real."

"Oh."

It's all I can say. I'm still recovering from the vision of his tongue and where I would like it to be—on me.

What is wrong *with me?*

"You said the other day that my teeth must all be fake."

"Did I?" I busy myself with a gulp of wine. "I don't recall that."

"No?" He watches me carefully. "It was right before you said that I'm overrated as a player."

This is not good. I reach for my wine, only to realize that I'm on E. I pointedly look toward Caleb, but he notices my searching glance and pulls his pint out of reach.

Spoilsport.

I sip my water instead like a true lady.

"So, Charlie," Gwen butts in, her chin resting on an upturned palm, "how's work been lately? Hard? Still thinking about quitting?"

Through sheer force of will, I do not grimace. "It's fine," I tell her with a toothy smile, "We're taking on a few new projects. Very, very busy. So busy I don't have time to think about quitting."

Duke is looking at me again. I can practically hear his thoughts—*"If you're so damned busy, then why the hell have you been harassing me on Twitter?"*

I desperately need more wine if I'm going to survive this dinner. Obviously I did not think this plan through. I wonder if anyone will notice if I head to the bathroom and don't return.

Gwen tilts her head to the side, fingers dangling over the rim of her champagne flute in a poised way that grates on my nerves. "I heard through the grapevine that *The Tribune* is on the verge of bankruptcy." She pauses almost deliberately. "That's where you are, right? *The Cambridge Tribune?*"

I hate the way she's watching me smugly. "It is," I grit out, "but, you know, *The Tribune* is on its way up the ladder."

"Is it?"

No. Which is why I'm being forced to reel Duke Harrison into this ridiculous setup. If I had my way, I'd send his PR agent an email with a request to set aside some time to answer my questions. He or she would say yes. Done deal.

Instead, he's told me "no" in five different ways. Sitting next to him only serves to remind me of the fact that I spent the last two nights tossing and turning in bed, thinking about what dinner with him would be like. And not like this fabricated double date—a dinner with just the two of us.

The corner of my mouth cramps from my too-wide smile. I push forth undeterred to prove to Gwen that I'm not some daydreaming journalist.

Even though I sort of am.

Duke, no doubt sensing that a fight is on the horizon, breaks the tension. "So, what's 'Charlie' short for?" He flags down the server and points to my empty glass. I almost weep with gratitude, even as I think that he must be up to something. "Charlize?"

I blink. "As in, Charlize Theron?"

Across the table, Gwen snorts derisively and I curl my hand into a fist against my thigh.

Caleb kicks my foot, disrupting any homicidal thoughts that may or may not have entered my head. "Both you and Charlize have blonde hair," he points out. I love him. I might love him more than I love his sister, and that's saying something.

"Hers is sleek. I look like a lion stuck its mane into an electrical outlet."

Duke chuckles. It's a deep sound that curls my toes in my shoes and reminds me of toasty fireplaces and crackling wood. It's the sort of chuckle that you want to hear up close and personal, with your cheek pressed against a solid, male chest, and that sexy laugh rustling the top of your hair.

I'm hopeless. Casey will have a field day when she hears about this disaster.

"Ooo, I've got it!" Gwen claps her hands together. "Charlie *Sheen*!"

Is.

She.

Kidding?

My toothy grin slips. Nothing like being compared to the "*Win*ning" King to make you feel less attractive as a woman. "It's actually just short for Charlene," I tell the table stiffly. "It was my grandmother's name."

Like a true friend, Caleb murmurs, "A beautiful name. Very ancestral."

Gwen doesn't bother to say anything at all, as she's now got her phone out and is scrolling through God-knows-what. Probably selfies, if I had to guess.

"I'm named after the Duke of Wellington. Duke Wellington Harrison. My parents are huge Anglophiles."

It's said so abruptly, so out of the blue, that both Caleb and I freeze as though we've suddenly found ourselves on a tightrope hoisted twenty feet above the ground. If someone were to tell me a month ago that I'd be having a legitimate conversation with Duke Harrison, I would have told 'em to lay off the coke.

But this is reality. We are *actually* sitting her with the

Boston Blades' first-string goalie, and while he's not exactly smiling, he's not frowning either. If anything, he appears . . . uncertain. A little embarrassed.

It's almost endearing.

He rubs the back of his neck awkwardly. "I'm talking about the English military general, not the entrée."

As if scheduled by the gods, our meals arrive and, sure enough, a Wellington is placed in front of Duke, whose cheeks are now roasting with color.

Pointing my fork at his plate, I say, "I like coincidences. Tell me, did you plan it?"

"Of course he did," says Gwen, who has switched her focus from her cell phone to the dainty salad placed before her. "Also, Duke, the *GQ* editor just sent me an email about a feature with them. They want a full spread. Next week."

The good humor on his face slowly seeps away. The broody frown is back. I'm not sure whether I should be disappointed or pleased. Except—*hold on now.*

I direct my attention to Gwen. "What is it that you do again, Gwen?"

Immediately I begin to pray. *Please no, please no, please—*

"I'm Duke's PR agent. That's how we met, actually. Duke's sports agent hired my firm, Golden Lights Media, and it was almost like love at first sight. We spotted each other after a game and, oh, it was just *magical.*"

"Gwen," Duke growls sexily, even if he is saying another woman's name, "we are *not together.*"

Despite his assurance that he and Gwen are not, in fact, an item, my stomach drops somewhere south of my feet. Perhaps to Hell. I risk a quick glance at Caleb, whose mouth is pursed tightly like he's holding back laughter.

This is worse than I expected.

I almost wish that Gwen and Duke *were* dating. I imagine it would be easier to navigate that mess than one in which

Gwen James is actually The Mountain's PR guru. There is absolutely *no way* she'll let him even speak with *The Tribune,* off the books. She already thinks the newspaper is going down the drain.

And, yes, she would be correct on that assumption.

But how can I compete with G-freakin'-Q??!

Sweat beads on my forehead and I feel a mite bit dizzy. The conversation calls for a response, but I have nothing to say.

Well, nothing besides: *fuck me.*

Since this is neither appropriate nor a reasonable response, I force a bright smile. "That's so . . . sweet," I grit out, none too gently stabbing a piece of my steak. "So, Duke, does that mean mixing business with pleasure is accepted within the Blades' organization?"

His frown deepens. "Gwen and I aren't—"

"What he's *trying* to say is that we're a team, Charlie. We look out for each other, and make a sound decision on whether a tabloid photo or an interview—*whatever*—is beneficial to Duke's overall career before rolling with it."

There's a hidden message if I ever heard one. I just haven't quite uncovered all of the subtleties yet. Somehow, I imagine that those subtleties are lined with unsheathed knives.

I put down my fork and knife. "So, an interview with a local news publication. Would that be completely off the table?"

Duke drains his beer.

Caleb excuses himself to make a "very important phone call."

And Gwen . . . Gwen just turns to me with such a serene smile on her face that I'm reminded of my twenty-one year old self, who thought Gwen James was the coolest girl ever. Thankfully, I no longer suffer from such delusions.

"Is that a hint that you'd like *The Cambridge Tribune* to interview Duke?" she asks smoothly. Her smile might be wide and guileless, but the same cannot be said for her narrowed eyes.

I hold her gaze. "It was just a thought. *The Tribune's* fan base doesn't read *Sports Illustrated* or other, more well known publications." I'm lying through my teeth, not that I care. "I just think that it would be nice for some of our locals to see a side of their favorite hockey player from their favorite newspaper."

"I don't think so." That's all she says before her phone rings and she's forced to step away from the table to take the call.

Which effectively leaves Duke and I alone, seated side by side.

We're facing a wall and neither of us turns to look at the other for long, heavy moments. Even so, I can feel his presence beside me as tangibly as if he'd pressed his knee to mine. I'm tempted to do just that, to slide my right leg just two inches over and touch him. But his body is rigid, his left hand curled tightly around the cutlery.

In fact, he might not be breathing.

"So," I murmur, taking a sip of my wine, "you and Gwen?"

He blows out a breath of frustrated air. "You're slick, Charlie Denton. I'll give you that."

I keep my gaze fixated on the wall. "Not enjoying our double date, Mr. Harrison?"

He leans forward and, oh God, his knee is now touching my bare leg. Shivers chase down my spine, and the thrill has nothing to do with the food in front of me and has everything to do with the man at my side.

"This date is a sham and we both know it."

"I don't know what you're talking about," I sniff. "Caleb and I—"

"Are not together," he finishes in clipped tones. "Let's not even pretend that he's remotely interested in you. I walked up to you both, and his gaze went immediately to my crotch."

Ah, hell. I can't even blame Caleb for that reaction. Anyone with a pair of eyes would have a hard time keeping their gaze above the belt when it came to the man seated beside me. Duke Harrison just has that magical effect on people.

"He swings both ways," I say, offering up another healthy lie. "Obviously he was just struck dumb by your presence."

"A presence you ensured would happen when you reached out to Gwen." His voice is a growl, and hearing it sends a flicker of awareness through my body. Is this how he sounds in bed?

I ignore the flutters in my belly. "Do you want me to be honest?"

The exaggerated wave of his left hand snags my attention, and I finally turn to him. He's already watching me, I find, and his blue eyes are nearly a dusky black. "That'd be a nice change of pace."

My eyes fix on his handsome face. "What's that supposed to mean?"

He plants a hand on the table and leans in, invading my personal bubble. This close, I can see that he has a scattering of light freckles spattered across the crests of his cheeks, as well as a deep, pink scar that extends from his left nostril to the corner of his mouth. My lips part on the breath I've been holding, and Duke's gaze drops down to my mouth.

"It means," he says in a low, rumbling voice, "that you play dirty."

"No, it just means that I play to win."

Almost despite himself, his mouth kicks up in a wry grin. "Like I said, dirty." He breaks eye contact and slouches back in his seat. "The answer is still no."

"Because Gwen said so?" Now it's my turn to plant my hand on the table and lean forward.

Chin tucked to his chest, he lifts his gaze to my face. That one look is potent. Sultry. Dangerous. It's a very obvious reminder that while he might be playing nice with me right now, this is a man who is generally feared on the ice.

I lower my voice, mainly to conceal the quiver I fear will emerge when I speak. The way he is affecting me is *so* not in the plan. "Is it because you do everything she says, even if you two aren't together? You sure she isn't secretly your girlfriend? Oh, wait, I do believe I hear wedding bells ringing."

He ignores my blatant taunting and plays it cool, reaching for his beer bottle and touching the glass to his mouth. He's on empty, if I recall correctly, but perhaps for the sake of our battle of the wits, he doesn't let on that anything is amiss. This almost makes me grin, because who knew little ol' Charlie Denton from Cambridge, Massachusetts, could throw off the big, bad Mountain?

"You were saying?" I prompt with a little *I've-got-this* grin.

"How badly do you want this interview?"

Badly. And now that I've had the chance to speak to him alone, I'm craving more contact. It's completely unreasonable, seeing as how we exist on two very different planes.

Him: professional athlete.

Me: struggling journalist.

Nevertheless, I tell him, "I'm not willing to go to jail over this, but yeah, I need this interview to happen."

His left brow arches high. "Even though I'm 'overrated'?"

Now my grin is full-fledged. "We're all overrated in some capacity, don't you think, Mr. Harrison?"

"All right."

"All right, what?"

He studies me as he takes another fake hit of his beer. It's still undeniably sexy, and I squeeze my knees together under the table. "All right, if you want this interview then—"

"Duke!"

It's Gwen.

I slide back into proper position on my chair, facing the wall like a naughty school kid caught breaking all of the No. 2 pencils. Almost simultaneously, Duke places the beer bottle on the table and resumes his muteness.

Gwen doesn't seem to notice, if the way she pauses to squeeze his shoulders on the way to her chair is any indication. She waves her phone in the air. "You will never believe who that just was."

"The pope," I say, cutting into my steak.

Her tone is snippy when she replies, "No, Charlie, it was *not* the pope."

"A shame."

I swear I feel Duke's knee jostle mine, but the contact is so fleeting it's possible that I've imagined the entire thing.

"*Anyway*, that was actually the sports editor from *The Boston Globe*. He gave a fantastic pitch." Gwen resettles in her chair and flicks her voluminous hair over her shoulders. "You know, Charlie, I have you to thank for this opportunity."

I don't like the sound of this. Sending a hasty glance over my shoulder, my thoughts head straight to Caleb. Where in the world did he disappear to? He's supposed to be my emotional support for the night. In other words, he's failing at pretending to be my beloved fake boyfriend. When I fail to spot him, I slowly bring my attention back to Gwen's face.

Smug.

If her expression had a name, it would be "Smug" with a capital S.

Still, I can't let her see how much she's getting to me. I

straighten my shoulders, tip my chin up and say, "You're welcome."

Her brows knit together in consternation. "In case you're wondering *how* you've helped this—"

"I'm not."

"It's because if it weren't for you, I would have told that editor no." Gwen offers up another too-sugary smile. "But it was *you*, Charlie, who just pointed out that locals want to have a piece of Duke. So, we're going to give it to them."

My heart flops over in my chest. "You're going to let *The Tribune* hold the interview?"

"What?" Throwing back her head, Gwen laughs. It's one of those delicate *ha-ha-has* that celebrities used to hand out in spades on *Oprah*, the ones that don't sound genuine. The ones you're convinced are practiced in front of the mirror to check the line of a neck, the squint of the eyes. Gwen's laugh is perfect.

Perfectly fake, that is.

"No, Charlie," she says, wiping an equally fake tear from under her eyes, "Duke will be doing the interview with *The Globe*."

Lovely.

CHAPTER FIVE

"*H*ow'd the double date go?" Casey asks me the following morning at work. "Did you land the interview?"

I let my head thunk onto my desk. "It sucked. Gwen's his PR agent."

"*What?*"

"I know." My forehead squeaks against the desk as I turn to look her way. "I'd say it can't get any worse, but, really, this is pretty much as bad as it can get."

"Did you have the chance to ask her about *The Tribune* doing a feature on Duke, at least?"

"She said no."

"Damn," Casey says with a shake of her head. She sticks her pen in her mouth, chewing on the cap. It's a habit that she can never kick once she's in deep thought. Her desk is littered with teeth-imprinted pen caps. It's a little disgusting, but who am I to judge?

After a beat of silence, she adds, "Well, it was a good idea. On to the next, I guess."

On to the next.

The words ring hollow in my ears. Realistically, I know that missing out on an interview with Duke isn't the end of the world. My brain knows this. I can't say that my heart recognizes this truth, though.

A knock comes at the door and I lift my head from my desk. Josh, *The Tribune's* editor-in-chief and CEO, is standing in the entryway, shifting his weight side to side on his feet. He's an edgy sort of guy, and by edgy, I'm not talking about his personal style. He's a constant bundle of untapped nerves in a short, squat body.

As for the personal style part, that's pretty much nonexistent. Everyday is a cycle of cargo shorts, beaten up sneakers, and a different color polo T-shirt. Usually stained with whatever lunch he scarfs down that day—the polo, I mean.

"Need something, Boss Man?" I ask. Josh never shows up to our office unless something is on his mind. Sometimes, when we're lucky, Casey and I go weeks without making any contact with him.

Now, to my misfortune, he steps past the threshold and pulls his Red Sox baseball hat farther down over his bald head. "Denton, what's going on with that 'special piece' you were blabbing on about the other day?"

Ah, crap. He's talking about the Duke exclusive. "Oh, you know"—I run my fingers through my hair and my nail catches on a curl—"it's going. It's going *great.*"

The line of his mouth lifts with hope. "How great?"

I grapple for a believable lie because who am I to be such a hope-killer? "I'm almost done. Maybe just one or two more paragraphs left; some editing."

"That's it?"

"Yup!" My voice emerges on a high-pitched squeak. I sense the onslaught of Doom approaching quickly.

"I'd like to see what you've got so far. Maybe we can

squeeze it into tonight's edits, so it can go live tomorrow on the website."

I'm nowhere near complete. Hastily, I scan the papers on my desk, praying that I've got something on hand that I can thrust forward as an almost completed project. The sheets fly out from under my palm, drifting down to the floor like my soul.

I've got nothing.

I am so screwed.

"You know," I say, still fervently searching for *something* that can save my butt from getting the boot, "maybe it'll be best if it's a surprise."

Josh's brows furrow. "I don't like surprises."

Yes, I want to shout, *we all know how the editor-in-chief hates surprises*. Once, when I first was hired, I walked into Josh's office to find him turning his socks inside out to, and I quote, "Keep Lady Luck with him during his annual dental exam."

Give me a scientific study explaining how inside-out-socks statistically make a visit to the dentist suck less, and I'm right there with you. Until then, no.

I give one more pass over my unorganized mess and sigh. There's no way I'm climbing myself out of this hole. This is it, I can feel it in my arthritic left shin. The moment I'm fired. "Josh?"

He pushes his Sox cap back on his head, all the better to stare me down. "Yes, Charlie?"

"I lied, just now."

Casey gasps and then promptly rushes from the room.

Traitor.

Arms crossing over his square chest, Josh takes another step into our 1970s replica office. "I know, Charlie."

I blink. "You do?"

"You're a shit liar," he informs me with a nod. He invites himself to Casey's lumpy chair, acting a little surprised when he sits and the chair protests with an audible *creeeeek*. "You've always been a shit liar. Remember when I first hired you and you swore up and down that you'd personally interviewed Tom Brady?"

"Now, I didn't say *that* exactly." My wince is the stuff of legends; it cannot be concealed. "I'd said that I had interviewed Tim Brady, former Boston University hockey player. Minor difference."

My interview with Tim Brady had taken place at a college frat party with BU's golden hockey boy head first over the toilet. As Tim had prayed to the porcelain gods after way too many rounds of Jagerbombs with his teammates, I had questioned him on his stick play, his love for the penalty box, and why in the hell he'd decided to screw the coach's wife.

The meat of the story, ladies and gentlemen.

Never let it be forgotten that Charlie Denton didn't pull through for journalism.

Regardless, Josh is not looking so appreciative at the moment. His hat is resting on his knee and the fluorescent light is reflecting off his shiny head. "You said you interviewed Tom Brady," he clips out.

I hold up a finger. "*Tim* Brady," I correct pleasantly. "Trust me, I wish I could pull off an interview with the Patriots' G.O.A.T."

Josh's knee bounces up and down, and he actually bites his lower lip like he really wants to tear me a new one, but is reviewing *The Tribune's* HR policies in his head. Then, almost without warning, he blurts out, "Duke Harrison."

"Excuse me?"

"Duke Harrison," he repeats, slapping his Sox hat back on his head and pulling the brim low again. "We talked about doing a feature piece on him. Well, now I want you to interview him personally."

I blindly reach for my coffee mug only to remember that I

drained the last dregs over an hour ago. "You do realize that it'll be pretty difficult to nail that down, right?"

Josh presents me with his back as he heads for the door. "I'm aware," he throws over his shoulder nonchalantly.

My hands go to my desk for leverage as I stand, so that I can see him over the desktop monitor. "You're *aware* that it might be difficult?" I try to keep my voice level, I really, really do, but I'm also internally panicking. I've been hounding Duke for days now, to no avail. And that was *before* my boss decided to officially assign me the story I was already chasing. "What if I can't make it happen?"

He pauses. Twists around. "The same way you couldn't make that interview happen with *Tom* Brady, NFL megastar?" This time, Josh doesn't even wait for my response. "If this interview doesn't happen, then you're not a real sports journalist, Charlie."

"Josh," I say slowly in a tone that's mostly reserved for dealing with wayward children on the verge of a temper tantrum, "I'm not sure what's changed from yesterday. I'm going to get you that article, I promise. I'll whip something up, get it prepped. You'll have it by three p.m. this afternoon."

"The Duke Harrison feature," he announces curtly. His face is a mask of ambivalence and I'm more than positive that mine is red and blotchy from sudden stress. "I'll be nice and give you until next Friday. That's all of eight days from now."

Eight days. I have eight days or . . . I gulp back my fear and ask, "What happens if I don't make the deadline?"

Josh straightens out the brim of his hat like he means business. "You'll be demoted."

"To *what?*" There's nothing below me. It's not like *The Cambridge Tribune* is teaming with interns. Each "department" is bare bones. Hell, we clean our own offices—or, we did, until the vacuum broke. I suspect even the vacuum couldn't take the 70's throwback décor anymore.

"You'll be my secretary."

My mouth drops open at Josh's words. I can honestly think of nothing less I would rather do than to be his go-to grunt girl. His last three secretaries have quit within a week. Not, however, because he's demanding, but rather because he grows a bit too touchy-feely during late work nights.

Rumors spread.

I'm not about that life.

"Josh," I try again, giving one more go at reasoning with the man who's universally known among the office staff for being *un*reasonable, "Let's think this over, maybe? How about we let go of this Duke thing and go for someone more realistic, like someone on the . . . the Kennedy High School's basketball team. I can swing that, easily."

"No."

Would it be too embarrassing if I cry right now? I think it just might be.

Josh turns for the door one last time. "It's Duke Harrison or nothing, Charlie. Oh! And before I forget, I recommend that you stop using your work computer for job hunting. It's against company policy."

And with that, my boss struts his way out of the room. I promptly drop to my chair, ignoring the way it jerks and twitches under the sudden onslaught of my weight. I do, however, gird myself for abruptly falling to the floor.

When it seems that I'm safe for yet another day, I stare sightlessly at the computer. Sure enough, I actually have the Careers page pulled up for *The Boston Globe*. I wouldn't think that Josh is smart enough to have my Internet browser tracked, but clearly I'm wrong on that score.

I should probably tell Casey to stop checking her online

dating website, but since she skipped out and left me to the wolves, I'll hold off . . . for now.

So, it has come to this: Duke Harrison or becoming Josh Wharton's office bitch. If there was ever any doubt in mind about what moves needed to be made next, none of it still exists in the aftermath of my conversation with Josh.

I snag my phone from its place in my top drawer and open the Twitter app. Duke's message about me having a good day is the last one that came through. Not. Any. Longer.

My fingers fly across the touchscreen, and this time there's no deliberation. I hit SEND within fifteen seconds and then stare down at the words:

I need that interview. Name your price.

CHAPTER SIX

"*This* is where we're discussing terms?"

I hiss the words at Duke's broad back as I follow him down a dark, dank hallway. I've lived in Cambridge for my entire life, and yet have never known this place even existed.

"Dive bar" doesn't even begin to adequately describe the state of The Box, a name I'm presuming derives from the "penalty box" in hockey. I could easily be wrong; perhaps it's referring to the almost cage-like, prison-y vibe this hallway is giving off. I'd say that it's a cross between traditional English pub and local neighborhood bar, but honestly? That would be giving this place way too much credit.

Then my mouth nearly drops open when we pass a life-size wax figure of Bobby Orr, the best hockey player to ever exist, as well as a hometown hero here in Boston. Naturally, I have to touch it.

"Charlie, hands to yourself," Duke grumbles ahead of me. He must have eyes in the back of his sexy head. How else would he know that my fingers are mere inches away from landing on Bobby Orr's wax nose?

I skip ahead a step to catch up. "Seriously," I say, infusing as much authority as I can into my voice, "We could have discussed everything over the phone. When I said 'name your price,' I didn't mean that you had the right to kill me. This place looks like something straight out of the Investigation Discovery Channel."

"I'm not going to kill you." He says this with a shake of his golden head, like it's the most ridiculous thing he's ever heard.

"Obviously not. If you did, your career would be over. Not even The Mountain can escape—"

My voice cuts off as my gaze lands on another figure, and this one looks incredibly familiar. Golden hair. Robin's egg blue eyes. Thin scar. Sharp jawline.

My eyes widen when realization strikes.

Holy. Cow.

"Duke," I say, "Do you seriously have your own wax figure?"

This time when I reach out, my fingers hit cold hardness. As expected of a wax figure, not real flesh.

What's not expected is the way Duke's fingers snag my wrist and pull my hand away from his likeness. "I said, don't touch."

His mouth is frowning, handsomely sullen. I'm struck with the sudden urge to run my fingers across *his* face, just to see if he is as warm as the wax figure's face is cold. But there's something more to it, too; I'm practically itching to discover more about this elusive man, a man who lives in the spotlight but who, aside from his rarely touched Twitter page, hasn't left much of a personal imprint on the Internet. In today's day and age, such a feat is so incredibly rare it might as well be extinct.

Slowly, I become aware of our closeness in the dimly lit hallway, and my breath catches. Shadows dance across the masculine planes of his face, hollowing out his cheeks and slashing across his full, unsmiling mouth. He doesn't release my hand, at least not right away. Instead, his thumb swipes down, over the heart of my pulse. It's barely a caress, but it feels . . . telling.

Of what's to come.

Don't be an idiot, Charlie.

Right. Nothing is happening between Duke and I, even if his blue eyes do appear warmer in the dark. And even if his thumb has now started a soft back-and-forth motion across the width of my wrist that has my knees wobbling with desire.

I mentally pull myself together with the reminder that if I do not make this interview, my butt is toast. Giving a little tug of my hand, his fingers fall away as though they were never there in the first place.

Cradling my hand to my chest, as though he's done irreparable damage to it, I murmur, "You didn't answer my question."

The groan he gives me is low and sexy. "You ask too many questions."

"Hey, it's not my fault. We're standing next to your own *wax figure* and you don't think that's weird."

"I've walked past it hundreds of times."

"Okay, well, why is it here?"

"The owner is a hockey fan. You'll see."

Turning on his heel, he continues down the same dark path that seems to stretch on for forever. In reality, we walk for perhaps another ten seconds before he raps his knuckles on a wooden door and swings it open.

I blink.

Then, I physically ball my hands into fists and rub my eyes because surely I'm not staring at the Blades hockey team shooting the shit over pool tables, and lounging out on the couches.

"What *is* this place?" I whisper in awe.

"The Box."

"Yes, I read the sign at the front of the building." I wave my arm at the sight before me. "But why am I staring at your entire team?"

With a hand to my lower back, Duke moves me to the side so he can shut the door behind me. I can feel that large hand of his like a permanent imprint to my skin, even after he's stepped away and opened the distance between us.

"The Box is split up into two separate bars," he tells me. "Front of the house"—he jerks his thumb toward the door we just came through—"and back of the house for us. The owners are huge hockey fans, and they've been operating this place since the 80's, at least." He offers a roll of his shoulders. "Sometimes it's nice to just relax and not have to worry about the media hounding us."

The look he gives me indicates that he's talking about me and me alone. I flash him my toothiest smile and he glances up to the ceiling. Probably begging the Heavens to take me off his hands.

Eight days, I want to tell him, *you have me for eight days*.

"So, what, you guys just camp out back here, hiding from us plebeians?"

"Something like that." The corners of his mouth lift, and damn, but his smile is sinful. Fake tooth and all, this man is a walking billboard for sex. Then, he breaks the spell, gesturing for me to follow him to the bar.

We catch a few side-eye glances and I return them fully. I can't help it. I'm a hockey junkie and I'm in a room with some of the best players in the NHL.

Baylor "Zombini" Jeffs.

Ryan "The Hitter" Markssen.

Andre Beaumont.

This is nuts, totally mind-boggling.

Duke doesn't take the free barstool. He invites me to it with a dip of his chin, and I casually take the offering, as though a professional hockey player giving me his seat is regular scheduled programming in the life of Charlie Denton.

It's not, and I thrust away the unbidden thought that this feels a lot like a date.

As he waits for the bartender to come our way, he removes his leather wallet from his back pocket and idly taps the worn corner against his palm. "You look awestruck."

There's no point in lying. "A little bit, yeah."

His gaze cuts to mine, seeing through the layer of bullshit I'm offering up on a silver platter. "Just a little?"

"Okay, so I might be on the verge of a minor anxiety attack right now."

The air vacates the room when his blue eyes dip to my mouth and linger. "You gonna need mouth-to-mouth, Charlie?"

My breathing hitches. "You offering, Mr. Harrison?"

His eyes crinkle at the corners, and he turns away as the bartender finally approaches us. I fend off disappointment that he didn't respond to my attempt at flirtation. Not that I'm surprised, though. Flirtation and Charlie Denton aren't exactly synonyms.

"What are you two having?" the bartender asks, snagging two napkins from a black dispenser and popping them on the bar top.

"My usual," Duke says, then glances over at me. "What are you in the mood for?"

You.

Thankfully, for once, I don't voice my thoughts out loud. Quickly I scan the rows of glass bottles beneath the backlit wall. "Gin and tonic?"

The bartender doesn't even blink. "Lime or lemon?"

"Lime, please."

As he heads off, Duke returns his focus back to me. Seated as I am, I can't help but notice his massive size. I wasn't kidding when I said he was monstrous. For a goalie, he's got the right frame: tall and broad, lean. Today he's wearing dark-washed jeans and a soft-looking sweater, no hint of his tattoo in sight.

Disappointing, to say the least. I was hoping for another peek, shameless hussy that I am.

"What made you say yes?" I finally ask.

"To meeting here and discussing your interview?"

"Yeah." I thank the bartender when he delivers our drinks, and then stifle a pleased smile when I reach for my wallet and Duke makes a point of handing his credit card over. "I'm not complaining, but somehow I don't think that this"—I motion to the secret bar he's brought me to—"is what your 'price' is for helping me out."

He brings his beer bottle up to his mouth. "You're right," he murmurs in a gravel-pitched voice, "it's not."

"All right." I wrap my hand around my cocktail and take a sip through the short, tiny straw. "Then let me have it."

CHAPTER SEVEN

"*Y*ou ask questions on my time schedule."

I stare at a speck of lint on his sweater. Not because it's all that noticeable (it's not), but because I'm desperately attempting to riddle out his words. The overhead lights pitch darker, giving the bar a soft romantic glow though I must be the only female in the house.

The Box is proving to be a very intriguing place.

After sipping my gin and tonic, I ask, "Are you referring to scheduling the interview around your games, that sort of thing?" If so, I'm not sure what would make this any different than any other interview I've ever done.

My job at *The Tribune* might not come with prestige but I'm not incompetent. I'm on the verge of saying this to him when he shakes his head and murmurs, "Not exactly."

"Are you going to make me guess what you're talking about?" I fiddle with the straw in my drink, doing my best not to notice the way we've started attracting more attention from his teammates. Surprisingly, they stay away and give us space, though I feel them watching us.

He tilts his head just so, his blue eyes finding my face in the dim lighting. "I'll take pity on you. Give you a clue."

I roll my eyes. "How chivalrous of you."

"I can be chivalrous. When, and if, I want to be."

"That's like saying you can be kind, in between bouts of dickish behavior."

His laughter is contagious and I feel my lips tugging into an unexpected smile. Duke Harrison is a danger to anyone with a beating pulse, I decide. He's quiet and witty, mysterious and candid. It's a heady combination that I'm sure helps women lose their panties around him fairly frequently.

Hell, even my panties are feeling a bit loose right now, and that's a problem.

To get my mind back in the game, I force a churlish glint to my voice. "All right, just tell me." I make a come-hither motion with my hands. "I'm an adult; I can take it. Are we talking about trailing you from practice to physical therapy to whatever errands you've got tasked for the day? I can't say that the prospect of following you around is entirely thrilling, but for the sake of the story . . . I'll learn to be a Grade-A stalker. You'll never have to worry that I'm not there."

The guy on the stool next to me gives me a weird look, and immediately moves away. Seeing an opportunity, Duke hikes one boot onto the stool's foot rung and sits down. Without waiting for an invitation, he scoots the stool closer to mine, props his forearm on the bar top, and leans forward.

Suddenly, we're breathing the same air.

I'm fully aware of how utterly creepy that sounds, but it's so true. He's entered my personal space, though not in a way that's off-putting or uncomfortable. Instead, I'm filled with the urge to lay my hand on his knee or to wrap my hand around his bicep and tug him down for a kiss. I want to see if the scent of pine is stronger on his skin, and to deduce whether the fragrance belongs to his cologne or to his body wash.

Oh, boy.

I am *so* in over my head.

As I gulp down the last of my cocktail, Duke lifts a brow in response. "Need another?"

"No! I'm good."

His gaze falls to my empty glass. "Don't tell me you're a sloppy drunk, Charlie."

"Of course not." My tone is indignant. I can hear it over the heavy pulse of Avenged Sevenfold playing in the bar, and over the accompanying thunder in my ears. "Well, okay, I sort of am. I cry when I'm drunk. Awful, awful tears. Trust me, I'm cutting myself off at one drink more for your sake than for mine."

"I'm a big boy."

Naturally, my gaze falls to his crotch.

Naturally, he catches sight of this and, to my complete mortification, he touches a finger to the point of my chin and gently lifts. *Oops.* Caught red-handed. My gaze jumps away, landing on the bartender who's slinging two drinks at once. Impressive.

Duke's husky voice garners my attention. "Nothing to say to that, Charlie?"

Primly, I fold my hands over my crossed legs and flash him a smile. "You're slick, Duke Harrison, but I don't fall for high school tricks."

A throaty laugh escapes him, and he goes so far as to tip his head back and squeeze his eyes shut. Sue me, but I can't help but wonder if he looks just as hot when he's having an orgasm. I've never been one to ogle a guy so openly before— Duke is apparently my kryptonite.

Needless to say, when his laughter fades I'm left with damp panties.

It's tremendously unfair.

We need to get back on track before I'm tempted to do something stupid, like proposition a man who would never say yes to a woman like me. Thumping the bar with my closed fist, I exclaim, "Business, Duke. What're you talking about with this scheduling thing? Am I supposed to follow you everywhere? Stalk you to your apartment? Hide out in the locker room? I'd prefer to avoid arrest, just so you know."

He reaches for his beer bottle, and I watch as his throat works down the liquid. No wonder they chose him for the *Got Milk?* ad however many years ago now. He's still got it.

And by "it," I'm obviously talking about sex appeal.

"All right," he murmurs, dragging his hand through his hair, "We'll do this your way and refrain from breaking out the handcuffs."

Does he *have* to make everything sound sexual? It's a talent, I'm sure of it.

"This is the way your interview is going to go down." The tension in his wrist slackens, so that the beer bottle hangs loosely from his thumb and index finger. Bouncing the body of the bottle against his knee, he continues, "I'm not one for staged features, so if you want this, you're going to have to do it my way. I'll arrange when we can meet up, and I'll let you know when you have a chance to ask a question. One question per meeting. You following?"

My eyes narrow at his high-handed tone. "Your dick is showing," I say, holding up a hand when he arches a brow and glances down at his jeans. "*Not* that dick, Mr. Harrison. I'm talking about your glowing personality."

"I thought you wanted this interview?"

"I thought you were chivalrous," I counter with a smirk.

He shifts his weight and his beer bottle lands softly on my knee. With the cool condensation seeping through my jeans, I'm struck silent by the expression on his face. I have enough sexual experience in my pocket to recognize desire when I see it.

Now, whether it's a desire to strip me naked or a desire to bash the bottle over my head—that, I have no idea.

The bottle goes to the bar, abandoned, and Duke's hands land on the wooden legs of my barstool. When he drags the stool close to him, I let loose a startled yip and clap my hands on his shoulders.

"What are you *doing?*" I growl, turning my grip into two palms smacking his chest away.

"Being chivalrous."

"I didn't ask you to move my stool," I tell him, refusing to admit, even to myself, that my heart is pumping erratically in my chest. "In fact, I was fine just where I was."

He watches me silently, blue eyes hooded with an unreadable emotion. That one look entraps me, though, and I find myself leaning forward as if pulled by an invisible thread.

I swallow, hard. "I don't think you were being chivalrous," I say with false bravado.

"No?" His knee bumps mine. "What do you think I was doing, then?"

I edge closer, debating the merits of playing coy. Duke seems like a straight shooter. As much as I'd like to practice my sorely neglected flirting skills on him, I'm so not interested in throwing myself into the line of fire.

In a voice carved from gravel, he rasps my name. "Charlie?"

Don't fall prey to his good looks, don't fall prey to his good looks, don't fall prey to his good looks . . . "You're trying to distract me from my goal. I see what you're doing here."

"I don't think you know at all what my angle is right now."

I stare at him blankly. "What do you mean, *your angle?*"

His blue eyes find my face, and I'm struck with the realization that he's serious. Would I be crazy to think that he *actually* wants me naked? It's a wild, ludicrous thought, and I mentally shove it into a metal bin as soon as it manifests in my head.

"Duke . . . "

"Ask me your first question, right now."

It takes a moment for my brain to compute his words. "Are you referring to what's happening here, between us—?"

When I motion between our bodies, his latches onto his beer bottle and then drains the rest in one swallow. "No," he grunts, "Not this. Ask me your first question for the interview."

"I don't have my recorder."

"You have a phone?"

Oh, right. I fumble with my purse, muttering, "I'll have to download an audio app . . . "

"I'll wait."

He says it so succinctly, without nearly the same level of heat as he said my name just moments ago, that I feel decidedly chilled to the bone. He's hot and cold, fire and, well, ice. Like his Twitter bio, he's a man of few words. Somehow, it fits him.

As the app downloads, I flick my gaze up to him. "What if I don't have a question prepared?"

"You've got . . . " His finger taps my phone's screen to life. "Fifty-nine percent left to think of one."

"You're mad that I called you overrated, still, aren't you." It's not posed as a question. Nor does he rise to my bait. Instead he hails the bartender for another round, this time making our order two water bottles.

Chivalrous or not, I secretly like the fact that he's joined me on the sober train. I've never been a heavy drinker, preferring water or smoothies to booze.

Just as the bartender drops off our waters, the app on my

phone invites me to open it. Two clicks later, and I'm staring at a pulsing red circle, tempting me to begin the recording session. Deep breaths. Don't I want this?

Of course, even if I don't, it doesn't matter. Unless I want FIRED written across my LinkedIn page, this interview with Duke has to happen. Eight days. I'm hoping that he doesn't plan to string this process along for longer than that.

From my periphery I notice him twist the white bottle cap open. He does the same for my bottle and places it by my elbow.

I resist the urge to sneak a peek at his face.

"Okay . . . So, this is the first time I'm ever going into an interview with nothing lined up. Just being honest here."

Duke taps his water bottle to mine in a salute. "No time like the present. Hit me."

I deliberate on whether I should hit hard, a real body check, or if I should start slow and work my way up. The fact that I'm currently sitting in a bar full of Blades players is answer enough.

Aiming for a stint in the sin bin, it is then.

I tap the red button on my phone and the white numbers kick off . . . one second, two seconds, three seconds, more . . .

"At thirty-four years old, some might say that you're well past your prime for a professional goalie."

I glance up just in time to see him blink and look away. "Is that your question?" he asks flatly.

"Well, no."

"Gordie Howe played until he was fifty-two," he says with a bit of a defensive edge. "By that count, I've got nearly two decades left in me."

"I'd say the game was much different in 1966, wouldn't you?"

His gaze flicks to mine and I recognize the look there as surprise. "Didn't realize you'd know when Howe retired."

Now it's my turn to sound mulish. Same crap, just a different day. "I'm a fan of the sport, Duke, despite the fact that I'm a woman."

"I didn't mean to say—"

"That because I'm a woman, I wouldn't know hockey? I'm sure you didn't mean anything by it, but the implication was there." It's not the first time I've been on the receiving end of this assumption. It nevertheless stings a little bit each time. Hardening my voice, I fold my arms over my chest. "We'll move past it because I recognize that you're doing me a solid here. My point in bringing up your age was not to point out that you're old—"

"That's because I'm *not* old," he grumbles testily, grabbing for his water bottle.

"My point was that you've been off for three seasons now. Your goals-against-average has slipped dramatically, and there doesn't seem to be a link to a weak defensive line. In every other facet, the Blades are leading in the division."

"So, your first assumption is that my dinosaur-like age is holding back the team."

"No," I murmur, shaking my head, "My first assumption is that you've suffered an injury. But as no reports have surfaced suggesting that, and since you haven't missed a game except on second-string days . . . *Then,* I naturally proceed to my next suspicion."

"My age."

I give a little shrug. Perhaps I should have apologized in advance. I become something of a barracuda when I get in the groove, exhibiting the same level of tenacity as I once did on the ice back in the day.

"Here's my question." I turn to him fully, jumping only a little when our knees collide again, and I'm forced to rearrange myself. In doing so, my left knee slides between his thighs. We aren't skin-to-skin, thanks to the layers of clothing separating us, but I can feel the heat radiating off him in waves.

"Charlie?"

Stop imagining him naked. Right, right.

I briefly let my eyes fall shut, thankful for the dimly lit room, and then crank them back open. Game on. "The Blades aren't heading to the Stanley Cup this year, unless some sort of miracle happens. I'm hoping for it because I'm a diehard fan, but locals are trying to keep their heads on straight, myself included, and we aren't making any big bets."

His thighs squeeze mine, and I wonder if he's doing it on purpose to throw me off my game or if the topic of conversation is unnerving him. "Get to your point," he says before taking another hit of his water. "Please."

Such a gentleman.

"Sports analysts across the country are lining up to point out your whopping thirty-four years. They've griped about your old back injury, as well as the number of concussions you took early on in your career when you played right wing and not goalie. Lately, conversation has shifted from injuries and age to your free agency status at the end of this season. For the sake of my readers, I'm going to ask the question they most want to know: if offered a better deal elsewhere at the end of this season, will you be leaving the Blades?"

For a moment, he says nothing at all. In the silence, he finishes his water bottle and then reaches for my untouched one. Does he wish for something stronger? More alcoholic? Tough to tell. The tabloids hardly ever have a field day with him, and they've certainly never mentioned a drug abuse or alcohol problem.

Aside from the panty-dropping smile and its effect on women across the country, Duke Harrison has kept his nose clean over his decade-plus long career.

With a hand combing through his hair, Duke lowers his voice so low that I doubt my phone's recorder app will pick it up. "Free agency or not, I'll stay with the Blades as long as they'll have me. I signed on as a rookie with this team. I won my first Stanley Cup with this team. My second one, too. My past injuries notwithstanding, I've got nothing holding me back anymore." He pauses, dragging the silence on for another two beats, and adds, "So, feel free to tell your *readers* that I don't plan on leaving Boston until Boston kicks me out."

"Then what?" I ask, intrigued by the fiery passion in his blue eyes. This is the most I've heard him speak since we met last weekend. I don't want him to stop. I want to hear that passion wash over me, and soak up the determination he emits in spades.

Instead of answering, he reaches out and taps the red button on my phone to end the recording session. "No more questions for tonight."

Instinctively, I want to push him for another round. I want to crack the shell he's donned and dig around through the various layers. It's the journalist side of me, never being content with being told "no more" when it comes to a juicy story.

Maybe Casey is right. Maybe I should have become a tabloid reporter where juicy stories are the norm.

"Thank you," I tell him, because I'm genuinely grateful that he's even letting me interview him. I drop my phone into my purse and tug my coat tightly around my body. "Guess I should be heading out, then. Will you let me know when—"

"I have a question for you."

"I'm sorry, please repeat."

"A question for you."

I shake my head, sending my blonde ringlets flopping

about my face with the movement. "I don't think that was part of the original terms."

"I'm amending the terms right now."

I trail my gaze over his broad shoulders and up to his handsome face. His blue eyes are gleaming with a challenge. "All right. Give me your question."

"Do you like pizza?"

"Who doesn't like pizza?" I counter, laughing a little at the randomness of his inquiry. Where in the world is he going with this?

With a shrug, he says, "My brother, but it doesn't matter. I'd like to know . . . would you want to get some pizza with me?"

My body jolts with awareness, and I swear a tingle zips down my spine when he touches his knee to my leg again.

"Do you mean pizza right now?"

"Yes. There's a place that serves by the slice right around the corner from here. Maybe a five-minute walk, tops. Would you want to go with me, grab some late night dinner?"

All reason flees and I go with the first thought that enters my head. "I'd love to."

CHAPTER EIGHT

"*Y*ou look like hell," Casey tells me the next morning.

Still staring at my computer screen, I rub my middle finger along my hairline with not a drop of subtlety. "A compliment," I mutter dryly, "Hold me while I try to soak it all up."

Casey's laugh is loud in the quiet of the morning. There's no one here but us—if you don't count Josh, that is, who never fails to arrive before the crack of dawn. When I passed him this morning in the break room, he held up seven fingers and then strutted off like his job was done for the day.

Seven days.

"Seriously, though," Casey says, her chipper voice drawing my attention to her side of the room, "You've got bags under your eyes and your shirt is on inside out. What gives?"

I look down, peel my sweatshirt away from my skin, and, sure enough, there's the tag. No wonder I've been itchy all morning. I nod my head to the door, a silent command for

Casey to shut it. She takes obvious pity on me and does my bidding.

As soon as the latch clicks, I slide my arms through the necessary holes, twisting the sweatshirt around like I'm a pig in a blanket. The itchy feeling fades as soon as I stick my arms back out, and the collar of my shirt settles against my breastbone like it was designed to do.

"Charlie."

I sigh. "I met up with Duke last night."

Wait for it . . .

"You did *what?*" she shrieks, skipping to my side of the office where she parks her butt on a stack of papers on my desk. A few flutter to the carpet, forgotten. "How was it? Is he as hot in the sheets as they—"

My hands fly up in a classic time-out signal. "Whoa, now. We did *not* do any sheets sharing. We met up to talk about the interview . . . and then we grabbed pizza afterward."

Casey's brows waggle. "Is that what the kids are calling it nowadays?"

"We didn't have sex, Cass. Do you hear me? No. Sex."

Her elbow props up on her knee, and this new batch of shifting around sends another group of papers sailing to the floor. "Well, that's disappointing."

Since she doesn't seem to be inclined to pick up the mess she has created, I scoot back my chair and gather the loose leafs from the carpet. I drop them onto my desk, far away from her. "It's not that disappointing. Sex is not in our future. I need him for this interview."

"What does he need from you, then?"

Her question is one that's been darting through my head, too, for the last ten hours or so since we said our good nights. I've never been the sort of girl to make a move—I don't *have* moves—but I don't think I'm out of line in thinking that he was interested in more than just work stuff.

I mean, he asked me to dinner. Sure, it was a local pizza joint, but the cook knew Duke by name and made a fuss over me as soon as the bells chimed over our heads, signaling our arrival.

And the fact that he took me to a bar that caters to the Blades hockey team exclusively?

It's hard *not* to let my imagination run wild with an assortment of *what-ifs*.

"Maybe he's interested in you," Casey says, clearly over my stewing silence. "You're a catch, Charlie, and you don't even realize it."

Me? A catch? It's almost laughable. I'm not one of those women who sadistically gets off on putting herself down, but statistically . . . I've never been a "catch." Not in high school, when I suffered a bad case of unrequited love for my good friend, Adam. Cliché, right? Only this time around, Hollywood's favorite love trope did not work out in my favor.

We stopped talking right around the same time that I fessed up to my infatuation.

Then, there was that time in college when I gathered my courage to approach my crush. He'd played baseball for BU, and oh, man, but I'd lived to see him at games wearing his uniform. His butt? To die for, I'm not exaggerating. My bumbling question about us going out on a date together ended with him busting a gut, laughing. I prayed so hard that day for the ground beneath home plate to open up and swallow me whole.

My life is full of awkward instances just like these. Rinse and repeat.

Hope is a dangerous thing, something I've learned pretty well over the years. There's no way I'm bringing hope anywhere into the equation with Duke Harrison.

My phone buzzes with an incoming message and I reach

for it. A Twitter DM. My heart kicks into gear, fluttering in my chest.

"You okay?"

I ignore Casey's question and swipe at my phone screen to open the message from Duke.

Interested in catching the game tonight? I've got three tickets with your name on them. I'll answer one of your questions after I clean out the Red Wings on the ice.

There's no use in even pretending I don't know what game he's referring to. The Blades are up against the Detroit Red Wings tonight, and it's been one of the most highly anticipated matches all season.

After last year's playoffs, the Red Wings' primary center, Andre Beaumont, was traded to the Blades. I would have bought tickets myself but the price bypassed my *Tribune* budget.

When I speak, my voice is a bit rusty with shock. "You want to watch the Blades play tonight?"

Casey slips off my desk, taking with her another stack of papers. This time, she does the proper thing and picks up after herself. "Sure. Want to hit up our local? It's game day and you *know* they're gonna have those amazing BBQ jalapeño nachos tonight."

"No, I mean, do you want to *go* to the game. Like, physically call ourselves an Uber and head down to the arena to watch?"

My coworker's eyes go wide in understanding. "Oh. Oh, my God, um *yes*, I would love to go. How did you get tickets? Nosebleed seats were going for over a hundred bucks a pop last time I checked."

I hesitate in telling her the truth, but it seems that I don't have to. She claps a hand over her mouth, theatrically murmuring behind her splayed fingers. "Duke invited you?"

I nod, wishing that I could squash the ridiculous hope blooming in my chest.

I don't *do* hope, for a variety of reasons.

"Girl, I told you that he was interested in you. Don't even pretend otherwise."

"He's not," I protest weakly, because I'm not all that sure that I'm even telling the truth anymore. *Is* Duke Harrison interested in me? As unlikely as it seems, why else would he be going out of his way to invite me to pizza or to a game? Both activities, mind you, which have been on his dime.

I need to stay strong.

Even if I do re-read his message at least ten times (okay, fifteen) over the next few hours.

True enough to Duke's word, when Casey, Caleb, and I appear at the ticket-window at the arena later that night, there are three tickets waiting for me. I would have invited Jenny and Mel, but neither are hockey fans.

Not that Caleb is, either, but he's a total fan of hockey *players*, which counts in my book.

We shuffle quickly through the lines of people waiting, and then opt to grab some food from the concession stands before heading to our seats. While I go for a classic hot dog (ketchup and mayo, no relish), Casey and Caleb both purchase nachos drenched with every kind of topping known to mankind.

In fact, I'm not actually sure I see the chips at all.

If I had ever questioned their twinhood, my disbelief has now been suspended.

"I can't believe you're wearing that jersey," Casey says, shaking her head as we pluck our way through the throng of people.

"What? It's a free country."

I'm wearing a Red Wings jersey that my dad purchased for me the year before he was diagnosed with cancer. To this day, Frank Denton continues to be the biggest hockey fan I've ever known. Over the years, he made a point to purchase jerseys from every team in the NHL. As his only child, I've got them all. Tampa Bay Lightning. Chicago Blackhawks. Dallas Stars. The list goes on.

Naturally, I have a Blades jersey tucked away in the top drawer of my dresser, though it's not part of my inheritance from Dad. The Blades were a very new expansion team to Boston at the time of my father's passing.

However, in the spirit of "staying strong" tonight against the sexiness that is Duke Harrison, I pulled on my ten-year-old Red Wings jersey just before leaving my apartment this evening.

A girl's got to do what a girl's got to do, and all that.

There's a bit of surprise among us when we realize that our seats are just behind the net, giving us a full view down the rink.

"This is amazing," Casey whispers in awe as she takes her seat, "I've never been this close to the ice before."

Caleb sits on the other side of me, so I am sandwiched between the twins. "I have," he boasts, already digging into his nachos. "Remember that guy I dated a few months ago? Total Blades fan. If only he hadn't smelled like bad B.O, we'd still be dating."

I share a knowing glance with his sister. "Isn't that the same guy you cried over for two weeks? The one who broke up with you for snooping around on his cellphone?"

Caleb shoots me a dirty look. "I have no idea what you're talking about."

"Really?"

"Okay, fine. He didn't actually smell bad."

Casey plants a hand on my shoulder, pushing me back, so

she can see her brother. "You slept with his T-shirt for a month."

With a harrumph, Caleb mutters, "Are we going to watch hockey or what?"

And with that, we settle in as the players, one by one, come onto the ice. There's something about hockey that I find addicting. The easy answer is that I love the game itself, with all of its nuances and controlled chaos. The more complicated answer is that I love the swooshing sound of skates hitting the ice, the smell of popcorn and hot dogs saturating the air, the excitement radiating from thousands of people as the clock counts down to the moment when the puck drops to the ice and the action begins.

Seated behind the net for the Blades, I immediately spot Duke as he skates towards us. He doesn't notice me, I don't think, but I do catch the number twelve across his back as he turns away and drops a water bottle into the top part of the net.

Other Blades players take to the ice, all wearing the same navy blue and silver uniform. My hands delve into my over-the-shoulder bag, grabbing a notebook and pen. My scraped-clean Styrofoam plate goes between my feet on the cement floor.

The tension in the arena thickens as we all stand for the national anthem. The players take to their respective sides, and my gaze immediately latches onto Duke, who casually positions himself in the hole. His already big frame looks even more massive while wearing all the pads and gear. With his helmet shielding his head, he looks like a warrior ready to spar.

And spar he does.

The puck drops and the first period kicks off.

The next fifteen minutes aren't so good, not for the

Blades. They play sloppily, something that Casey and I rant about in between screaming at the ice.

"*Jesus Christ*, Holt, go for the fucking puck!" Casey shouts, banging her fists on the Plexiglas like a crazy lady when the Blades' left wing fails to connect his stick with the rubber puck.

I'm no better.

My notebook is forgotten on my seat as I cup my hands around my mouth and yell, "Stop playing a bunch of pansies out there!"

My comment is directed at everyone, and the guys behind us laugh and join in on the hollering.

Then, the Red Wings' forward shoots the puck into the five-hole, sailing right between Duke's legs into the net.

"Oh, *c'mon*," I grind out, before watching in fascination as Duke hooks his stick around the forward's ankles and sends him sprawling to his knees.

It's a dirty move, one that goalies sometimes play. But Duke has always been a clean player, preferring to play hard than to play cheap, so it comes as a surprise. Duke isn't the player who hooks his opponents' ankles. This isn't to say that he won't throw down gloves if the situation calls for it—some of his prior brawls on the ice have even made it into the top clips for ESPN.

This move is different, though, and even the sports commentator sounds a bit shocked when he announces, "And, woho-ho, Harrison pulls a clinger right there. Haven't seen something like that from the Blades' number twelve in a few years. Maybe the rumors are true . . . maybe Harrison is feeling the need to skip clean playing to stay at the top of his game."

The whistle blows, calling for a penalty that has the whole crowd roaring with jeers and boos. I see Duke's helmet tilt as though he's watching Andre Beaumont skate toward the penalty box—Beaumont will take a turn in the sin bin in Duke's stead, since as goalie, Duke can't do so himself.

But then he twists around. With a shake of his head, and a quick spurt from his water bottle, Duke lifts his gaze . . . and notices me.

I see his narrowed eyes through the cage of his helmet. At first I think that he's pissed about his lousy play, but then I realize that his gaze is focused solidly on me.

Blue eyes rake over my Red Wings jersey, slowly sliding upward until our gazes clash. His brows come together and he scrubs one hand over his mouth.

He's annoyed.

Probably both at the game and at me, for wearing the opposing team's uniform. I've chosen the enemy.

I'm not the only one who has noticed Duke's ticked off expression, because the guy behind me taps me on the shoulder and says, "You sure wearing that Red Wings jersey was the best decision you could have made today?"

I glance at Duke, at the way his mouth has now completely flat-lined as he glares at the stranger talking to me. "I'm sure it doesn't matter. It's not like we really know each other."

Casey has already filled in anyone who will listen about my predicament, much to my frustration. The beer has gone to her head, I think.

"It looks like Harrison wants to know you," the stranger tells me conspiratorially. I think his name is Matt, but that's just a guess. "Do you want to see if I'm right?"

I tear my gaze away from Duke, who still appears annoyed, to Matt. Max? Hell if I know. "What are you talking about?"

"Do you want to see if I'm right, about him wanting you," Matt clarifies with a wide grin. "I bet you a beer that he does."

"I bet you two beers that he doesn't." I don't drink beer, but I'm sure Casey will take my trophies should I win. Ahem, *when* I win.

"You're on." Elbowing his buddy out of the way, Matt climbs down onto our row, issuing apologies when he scoots Casey over to step up next to me. Matt and I are the same height, which is to say, he's shorter than average. Definitely shorter than Duke Harrison. I force myself to not look at the net and the man glaring at me.

"Ready to buy me that beer?" Matt says, hooking a gentle hand around my elbow. His messy brown hair hangs down over one eye. I'm pretty sure he's in college, which explains his to-hell-with-it attitude.

Since I have no plans to buy him anything, I cross my arms over my chest and lean back. "A kiss on the cheek," I inform him, "and then I'll pretend to give you my number. That's all you're getting."

His friends break out into laughter, thumping Matt on the back in solidarity. "All right, all right," he mutters, still smiling playfully, "I'll work with it."

With absolutely no lead-up whatsoever, he drops a kiss to my cheek and then hits up my other cheek like he's a European. Removing his phone from his pocket, he hands it over and goes for broke: "I'd actually really like to take you out. So, like, if you want to give me your real number that'd be cool."

Beside me, Caleb gives a hoot of laughter. "Smooth move, kid."

Oh, this is awkward. I give him back his phone, resisting the urge to run my hand over my jeans. "You're a bit young for me."

Matt presses a hand to his heart, all faux-dramatic and everything. "I'm twenty."

"You can't even legally order the two beers you promised me."

"Which is why I asked you to buy me one."

Casey joins in on Caleb's laughing fit, and I sort of want to stab both of them. "Not happening, Matt."

"It's Max."

"Whatever." I roll my eyes, then flick at him with my hands. "Return to your seat, young one. The bet is over."

"Is it, though? Take a look at Harrison."

At Matt's—erm, Max's—prompting, I twist around. Without realizing it, the game has restarted, fast-paced and furious. But while the other players are fighting over the puck at center ice, Duke's head is turned just slightly . . . and I have the weirdest feeling that he's itching to turn around and face off against *me*.

CHAPTER NINE

J don't hear from Duke after the Blades lose against the Red Wings.

Like the lame-o that I am, however, I force Caleb and Casey to stick around by the concession stands as I keep watch over my phone. Originally, the plan was for him to message me with a place to meet. After thirty minutes pass, and then another twenty-five, I'm forced to accept that our scheduled meeting isn't happening.

Not tonight, anyway.

"Can we go?" Casey asks, pointing at the time on her watch. "Even if he had to talk with the press, it wouldn't take this long."

It might, actually, but I let the argument drop. With a last glance around at the employees sweeping the otherwise empty concessions area, I stuff my phone into my purse. "Fine, let's head out."

I don't let them know that I have a plan.

Thirty minutes later, I'm back in the dingy hallway of The Box. There's not much light, just one or two overhead spot-lights to guide the way. I pass by Bobby Orr, this time giving in to my inner-child instincts by patting him on the shoulder. I do the same with the fake Duke Harrison, except instead I flick him in the center of the forehead.

Immature? Hell yes, but I'm also pretty annoyed that he ditched me tonight.

My eyes slowly adjust to the lighting and I catch sight of other wax figures. These ones are just as recognizable: Milt Schmidt, Cam Neely . . . Phil Esposito. Oh, wow. This dungeon-like hallway is sporting Madame Tussauds-like wax figures of every Hall of Famer that has ever played for a Boston pro-hockey team.

My steps slow as I take note of each player; the lifelike slope of a nose, the broken teeth, and even the receding hair-lines. Duke, I notice, is the only player from the Boston Blades, a franchise that, ten years ago, was nothing but an expansion team.

Now, the Blades are one of the hottest teams in the NHL, and even went toe-to-toe with the Bruins in the playoffs last year. It's a weird dynamic, having two pro-hockey teams, but one that the city of Boston has taken to like fish in water.

Bostonians are nothing but crazy sports fanatics, anyhow.

I spare Duke's wax figure one more glance and then continue on my way, barely leashing a screech when some-thing skitters across my foot. Holy crap, I do not do rodents. My legs propel me toward the entrance door to the back bar, and I fling it open like I've been chased by ghosties.

At least three Blades players stop what they're doing to stare at me, open-mouthed, and I give a small, *hey-there* wave. I'm still in my Detroit jersey, which is probably a mistake, seeing as how the Blades lost 3-2 this evening.

This is what I get for being impulsive again.

"Can I help you?"

I turn at the sound of the male voice, expecting to find a bouncer ready to grab me by the back of my jersey and throw me outside. Instead, it's one of the Blades' second-string players, Marshall Hunt. He's wearing jeans and a polo T-shirt, and an expression on his face that's one tick away from *who-the-hell-are-you?*

Uh-oh.

Uncomfortably, I tug at the hem of my jersey, wishing that I had taken a moment to plan all this out in my head.

"Ma'am?" Hunt prompts impatiently.

Here goes nothing.

"I'm looking for Duke Harrison. Is he here by any chance?"

"Who's asking?"

This time, it's not Marshall Hunt speaking but another guy. I don't recognize him, so I'm guessing he might be one of the team's staff members. He has that admin look about him: pressed chinos, starched button-down shirt, leather dress shoes.

I look from Mr. Admin to Marshall Hunt, debating on how I want to play this. This tête-à-tête could go a few different ways, all depending upon how I form my next few words.

I'm not given the chance.

Someone else creeps up to our little group, and this guy I recognize off the bat. Andre Beaumont, the former Red Wings player who was traded to the Blades after last season. The player who had the whole arena howling tonight when he made two assists for the only two goals on the board. He stares down at me over the broken bridge of his nose and I actually gulp. Beaumont is a bit . . . harsh, shall we say.

(Read: he's scary as all hell, singlehandedly disproving the stereotype that all Canadians are lovely folks).

"You're that girl Harrison had here the other night," he says now, dropping his elbow onto Mr. Admin's shoulder. Mr. Admin takes it like a champ, though he does wince when

Beaumont's elbow cuts a little too close to his jugular. Andre points a finger at me, waggling it around like I'm a naughty child bent on mischief. "The journalist."

"How do you know I'm a journalist?" The words are out before I can stop them.

"Duke mentioned you today." His gaze drops to my jersey, and his nostrils flare. "You have a death wish, Miss Journalist?"

"No!" I clamp my hands around my bag's thick strap to keep from slapping my fingers over my mouth. "The jersey, it's just a joke," I tell them. "I promise."

Marshall Hunt leans forward, one hand slipping into his jeans' pocket in a casual, *I'm-sexy* pose. "It's not funny."

I'm dead. My body will be found in a back alleyway tomorrow morning. I can already see the headlines: "*Unknown Journalist perishes at the hands of the Blades; it's suspected that the victim made the mistake of wearing the enemy's colors before entering the lion's den.*"

This was such a bad idea.

"You're right," I say, tentatively backing up, "It's not funny at all. I have no idea what I was thinking. In fact, I'm going to head out." I turn for the door, my hand already extending for the doorknob. "Thanks for this little talk. I promise to remember it forever and always."

I barely get the door before it clicks shut with a force that doesn't belong to me. Then, I get a hit of pine.

Duke.

"Still wearing that jersey, Charlie?"

The heat of his body warms my back, though I keep my gaze locked on the wooden door. Hot, unexpected anticipation curls through me. Let's face it: since I left the arena almost two hours ago, I've been waiting for this moment.

It's all for the article, I tell myself.

Realistically, I know that the only thing tying Duke

Harrison and I together is the interview. Romantically (i.e., not real life), I'm so attracted to him, that I'm not really thinking straight.

As in, there is no reason I should want to lean back into his arms right now.

No reason at all.

In a husky voice I barely recognize as my own, I murmur, "Thought you were reneging on our bargain, Harrison."

His hand curls around my wrist. He doesn't give me a verbal response, but with a slight tug on my hand, he's pulling me away from his teammates. Marshall Hunt whistles, and I swear I hear Andre Beaumont say something along the lines of someone being "whipped."

No one stops Duke's trajectory path.

We round a few tables, cut past the bar, and enter a back room, which seems to be a near replica of the main bar area. Dartboards line the walls and two sets of pool tables are positioned parallel to one another in the center. A few guys are lounging on a pair of couches in the corner, but with one glance at Duke and I, they leap up from their spots and vacate the room.

Maybe I should be nervous.

Whisper a prayer, that sort of thing.

Silently I pull away from Duke's grip and wander over to the dartboards. I've never been good, that's for sure, but that doesn't stop me from picking up a dart and testing the weight in my palm. The arrowed tip is heavy and cool against my skin. It gives me something to think about other than the hot guy watching me intently.

"You play?" His voice is cool as his long-legged gait eats up the distance between us.

I tap the shell of the dart against my open palm. "Depends on the day."

He takes the dart from my hand. "Is that a yes?"

"It's a sometimes."

His lips quirk up, just a little, at the corners. "I'll take a 'sometimes.' Let's play."

Panic turns my palms clammy. "I don't know the rules."

"I thought you sometimes play," he murmurs, laughter rich in his voice. When he spots my face, no doubt pinched with anxiety, he returns the dart to me, folding my fingers over its cool hardness. "We'll make up rules. Twenty-one rounds."

Twenty-one rounds? Does he want to be here for the rest of the night? I opt for sarcasm when I mutter, "You want to beat me that badly?"

"Gotta recoup my losses from the night."

It's the first time he's mentioned the Blades' defeat against the Detroit Red Wings, and my gaze slithers away with guilt for wearing the red jersey of the opposing team.

"This is how it will work," Duke tells me, already having bypassed his mention of the Blades' loss. He approaches the closest dartboard with a confident swagger that weakens my knees, before tapping his finger on the red center. "Each round, whoever gets closest to the bull's eye has the opportunity to ask a question. Any question."

"A question for my interview?" I ask, hardly able to restrain my excitement. "Thought you'd limited me to just one question per meeting."

"I've changed my mind for tonight."

My eyes narrow and I fold my arms over my chest. "You don't expect to lose, do you?"

"I don't lose, Charlie."

"You lost today." I pretend to think on it, tapping my chin, and go the whole nine yards when I cock my head and stare him down. "In fact, the Blades have lost the last four games. If anything, you are on a *losing* streak."

He doesn't rise to my bait, not that I expected him to.

85

Duke Harrison is much too controlled to fall prey to sharp words.

"One question per round, winner asks it. Can be about anything." He points the dart at me, looking so sexy in a black T-shirt and worn jeans that it hurts. His tattoo edges out from beneath the sleeve, covering the length of his left arm all the way down to his wrist. The black ink swirls this way and that, creating abstract images of light and dark spaces over his naturally tanned skin. Right now, he doesn't look like Duke Harrison, pro-athlete. He looks handsome and approachable, a regular Joe that just so happens to be a near-identical twin to the Hollywood actor Charlie Hunnam. "You got it?"

I nod. "I got it."

We take our positions, lining up for what might be the battle of the century. I know what I want—this interview; him—but his motives are unclear. For all I know, he could be gathering intel on me so that he can slam me in the media's headlines.

"You want to go first?" he asks, holding out a dart. "Ladies first."

Nope. No way am I taking the bullet first, especially as I haven't thrown a dart since my last year of college. I need to work my way in to this, start slow and methodical. "Age before beauty, right?" I gesture at him with my hands. "You go first."

His mouth twitches, and he slowly shakes his head. "Subtle, Denton, real subtle."

Black sneakers toe up to the line. His hand raises, dart clutched loosely, and he bites his lip as he takes aim and fires. I'm so distracted by the curve of his hard bicep and his sexy tattoo that I hardly notice him clap his hands together in victory.

My gaze shoots to the board, and, sure enough, he's

scored a full fifty points. I wouldn't be surprised if the dart's tip hasn't plowed through the board itself, his aim was so precise.

There's no way I'm going to hit the bull's eye to tie him.

As I've never been someone to throw in the towel, I put an extra sway in my step as I grab for an extra dart. "Beginner's luck, right?" I ask over my shoulder as I position myself on the line.

Duke gives a soft chuckle from behind me. "Sure, Charlie, beginner's luck."

I screw my eyes shut, take a deep, mobilizing breath, and stare at the board. Might as well go for broke. I fire off the dart—

It bounces off the metal rim and clatters to the concrete floor, an echo so loud that I can hear the sound ringing in my ears.

Duke's already there, swooping up the dart. He turns to me, his blue eyes gleaming with laughter. "Might need to buy you a serving of Beginner's Luck from the bar. What do you say?"

I'm not a good loser, and I grumble a bit when I snag the dart from his grasp. "The dart's faulty."

His rich laughter curls around me like a warm blanket on a cold, cold night. "Your aim's the faulty one."

I roll my eyes, not willing to lose my bravado. There's a good chance I'll be losing every round tonight. "Just ask your question already."

"Fine." Retrieving his winning dart from the wall, he fingers the tip casually. "Why are you wearing that Red Wings jersey?"

"My dad bought it for me before he passed away."

His expression turns somber, the twinkle in his blue eyes dimming. "I'm sorry," he murmurs, "Was he a Detroit fan?"

I hold up a finger. "That's two questions, Duke. You scored only once."

With a shake of his head, he lets me evade answering. I appreciate it more than he'll ever know. After my dad passed away, my life teetered on the edge of uncertainty for a while. Did I attend university, like I'd always envisioned? Did I pick up whatever job came my way, just so that I could afford to pay the bills? Jenny and her family, lifesavers that they are, came to my rescue, offering me her family's couch to crash on while I figured everything out.

Within six months, I'd sold my family home so that I could afford tuition at Boston University. Sometimes, I still drive past our old house in East Cambridge, pulling up to the sidewalk so I can stare at the brown triple-decker and immerse myself in the memories.

But whereas the memories I've always been able to carry with me, the house funded my education. It's what Dad would have wanted, though that didn't make my decision any easier.

"You go first this time," Duke tells me, a hand lightly touching my shoulder as he comes around to my other side. One peek at his face confirms my fears: he knows that he struck a nerve with his question and wants to distract me.

Against my better judgment, I give him a grateful smile.

This round goes much the same as the first one, and by that I mean, Duke wins by a landslide and I'm forced to answer another question.

"Why did you want to become a journalist?" he asks, leaning against the pool table, his long legs outstretched before him.

"I like to pester people."

He catches my sarcasm, and points the sharp tip of a dart at me. "Give me the real answer."

I sigh. If I manage to lose every round, he'll know my

entire life story by the end of the night. "I've wanted to be a journalist since the time I realized that while I was good at sports, I wasn't the best. When I was on the ice, I had heart, and, yeah, I was in the top percentile when it came down to stats. But I wasn't good enough for anything beyond college hockey, and I had no interest in coaching. Sports journalism seemed the next best thing, a way for me to still be in on the action."

"On the ice?" His brow furrows in thought. "You played hockey?"

I let this second question slide. "Since I was six years old. Sometimes, when I have time, I still hit up rec leagues, but it's been a while. Works gets in the way." I flash him a shy smile. "Adulting, you know? It's a nuisance."

He still seems fixated on the fact that I once played hockey, and I note the way his gaze skims my body, taking in the thick thighs, the strong mid-section that doesn't nip into a teeny, tiny waist. Although it's been years since I played regularly, my body has never lost the shape of a powerhouse athlete.

It's safe to say that I am no Gwen James, who has the body of a Victoria's Secret model.

When his gaze lifts to mine, his eyes are smoky, nearly black. "We should play some time. See what you're made of."

The air between us thickens. My heart pounds in my chest. I need to pull myself together, now. Flicking my hair back in a move that belongs on the big screen, I reply, "Wouldn't you know, Duke Harrison, but I'm made of victory. Let's do this next round."

We keep pace with each other, though I lose more often than I win. He asks me frivolous questions—what's my favorite book, movie, song—in between more serious ones. I tell him about my mother leaving when I was young, and my struggle at work to be seen as a successful sports journalist in my own right, despite the fact that a penis does not dangle between my legs.

On the few occurrences where I beat him (and I'm convinced that he lets me win), he opens the door on a few secrets of his own. He admits that his parents never come to his games, as he's from upstate Minnesota and his mother is deathly terrified of flying. He assures me, however, that they've never missed a game on TV, and that they often blow up his phone while he's in the net, so when he gets to the locker room, he can hear their screams/excitement/joy in real time when he plays back their voicemails.

I learn about his brother, who played hockey in high school and college, but wasn't good enough to be picked up by the NHL. His brother is older, and for a few years in the beginning, they rarely spoke because, in his words, "It took a while for my brother to get his head out of his ass and let the jealousy go."

As each round presses on, Duke and I slowly eliminate the distance between us. His fingers linger when I take the dart from his hand. My hand brushes up against his back when I amble toward the board to tally up our scores. His hip softly taps mine when I actually manage to win three times.

Make that four.

Duke groans when my dart skirts closer to home base, and though I know he's exaggerating for effect, I can't help but do a little victory dance, throwing my hands in the air and stomping my feet.

"Another point for Charlie Denton!" I exclaim, making pistols out of my hands and blowing off the imaginary smoke from my index fingers. "Your turn to fess up, Harrison."

He throws up his hands, a wide smile on his face. "Give it to me, girl. What you got this time?"

His tone is nonchalant, but the heated look in his gaze is

anything but easy. For almost an hour, we've been doing this little dance and I have no idea what it means. I should be focusing on the job at hand, gathering information that I can use in my feature. I have one week to get that article on Josh's desk. Seven days.

But, like every other question I've posed to him tonight, I don't choose one that directly links to his career. Instead, I find myself asking the one question lurking in my conscious that just won't quit.

"What's going on with you and Gwen?"

Duke has been relatively chatty for the whole night, despite the way it started off, but at the mention of his Public Relations agent, he clams up and his blue eyes slide away. "I don't know what you mean."

I pluck the dart out of his hand, so he's not tempted to progress on to the next round. "Sure you do," I say brightly, wishing that I didn't sound so . . . fake. "Obviously something happened with you and Gwen at some point, otherwise she wouldn't have this perception that the two of you are an item."

When he gives a groan this time, I know he's about to dish the dirt. His hand rakes through his hair, then clamps down on the back of his neck. "We went on a few dates."

My heart plummets and I remind myself that *I do not care*. "Mixing business and pleasure must come naturally to you."

I don't necessarily point out that I'm referring to the two of us, and our little game of Twenty-One Questions. He catches my drift and frowns. "We went on those dates before my sports agent hired her to handle the press."

"Oh?" I hate how hopeful I sound, and I hide my pathetic bent by squinting at the TV in the corner of the room. The news cuts to a replay of Duke letting in the first goal of the night between his legs. I grimace at the sight.

"Two dates," Duke continues, our game all but forgotten.

"Somehow she's gotten it into her head that because we work together now, we're something more than we are—than we've ever been. Not to mention that those dates came months before I even saw her at that fundraiser."

At the mention of the fundraiser, I turn back to him. "Didn't she say that you two met there?"

His broad shoulders lift in a shrug. "She's crazy. She also frequently asks my sports agent out on dates, even though he's got a long-time girlfriend."

"Then why keep her around?" I ask, because the question is already there on the tip of my tongue. No use holding it back, since he's opening up and I want to know the answer.

"Honestly?" Duke rubs the back of his neck again. "She's damn good at what she does, probably the best in the Northeast. She might be certifiably off her rocker, but no one doubts that she's good at her job. And since my career, as of late, hasn't been . . . "

"Hot?" I offer, immediately wishing I could snatch the word back.

He pauses, dropping his eyes to his sneakers, before releasing a deep sigh. When he looks up at me again, his gaze is a little less bright. I feel the regret tugging at my lungs, stealing the breath from my body. "Yeah," he mutters bitterly, "A little less hot. Anyway, for all of her other faults, Gwen has been good to me. Good for my career, especially in the last two years since she's come on board."

I want to apologize, but something tells me he wouldn't appreciate the sentiment. Still, there's one last question burning on my tongue, and I give in pathetically. "Do you still go on dates with her?"

If I thought he looked upset before, now he looks downright annoyed. A pulse leaps to his jaw, ticking away like a sand-timer.

Without warning, he moves swiftly, invading my personal

space, backing me up against the wall. The dartboard is just to my right. His hands land on either side of my head, boxing me in until all I can smell is the scent of pine and all I can see is the ink peeking out from the neck of his T-shirt at his throat.

I inhale sharply, dragging much-needed oxygen into my lungs.

"You're not asking me about dating, are you, Charlie?" One hand slides down my arm before taking a detour and landing flat on my belly. The heat of his palm seeps through my layers of clothing. The heat of his palm sends want spearing down between my legs. "No, you're not asking me about dating," he rasps, his mouth dipping to hover by my ear, "You want to know if I fuck her, don't you."

"No," I whisper on a shaky breath.

"Liar."

He's totally right. I'm lying between my teeth. It's not my fault. I *do* want to know if there's something going on between him and Gwen, not that is affects me either way. Duke and I . . . whatever *this* is, isn't permanent. I have seven days until my article is due for review. Seven days to remember that my attraction to him is probably only skyrocketing because of close proximity.

If I only had to see him via TV or online, no way would I be suffering this sort of need. And, yeah, I'm needy. My hands are curling into fists, desperate to sink into his soft T-shirt and pull him close. My knees are stick-straight, to keep my body from sinking against his chest. My heart is beating so fast that I'm worried it might leap out of my chest.

I want Duke Harrison.

Maybe it's because of my job.

Maybe it's because he's the hottest guy I've ever talked to personally.

Maybe it's because whenever he steps close, all good reason flies away to destinations unknown.

Whatever "it" is, I give in to temptation and ask, "Are you having sex with her?"

I feel the vibration of his harsh laugh reverberate against my chest. "I don't mix business with pleasure, Charlie."

At the squeezing of my heart, I glance up to meet his gaze. "Then what are you doing right now?"

Just like that, Duke releases me with a curse. His hands fly to the back of his head, like he's got to keep them away from me. After a moment, in which my breathing slowly regulates and I've slumped against the wall for stability, he twists around. He points his finger at me, and then points at himself. "This isn't happening."

Disappointment grips my limbs, dragging my shoulders down in a hunch. "I got it. You, athlete. Me, nobody. You don't have to act so disgusted by the thought of kissing me."

His large hands follow the line of his neck and close down at the base. Stupid me, I can't help but notice how attractive he looks, all frazzled and disjointed. His biceps coil under his shirt, unfurling when he drops his arms to his side on a heavy exhalation. "It's not like that."

"Sure it is," I say, straightening my spine and snapping to my full height. I may want him, but I've got standards. Plus, it's not like I haven't been in a similar position before. Men never seem to want the goods when I'm ready to give them up—hence, my lack of a sex life.

Pushing away from the wall, I stalk over to the couch where I draped my coat an hour ago. I stick my arms through the appropriate slots, determined to not let him see how much his rejection hurts me.

"Don't worry about it," I tell him, zipping my coat up to my chin, a modern-day version of body armor. "You know what? Message me your email on Twitter. I'll forward the rest of my questions to you there. As long as I have them by next Wednesday, I'll make my deadline. Then, I'll get out of your hair."

Duke makes a grab for my hand when I stalk past him, whirling me around until I'm back in the same position—my back against the wall, the dartboard to my right. This time, I can't really feel the heat of his body, thanks to the thickness of my puffy winter coat.

"I'm not disgusted by the thought of kissing you," he mutters, his long-tapered fingers fluttering over my face, before cupping my head. His thumbs fan out over the crests of my cheekbones. "This has nothing to do with Gwen. Nothing to do with you."

"Exactly," I exclaim, slapping at his hand though he barely budges. "This has nothing to do with me. We've broken your rules, anyway. You said one question per meeting."

"I adjusted the rules."

"Then adjust them completely. We don't meet up after this."

He doesn't pull away, and I'm ashamed to admit that my heart rate kicks up speed again. Stupid, stupid heart. Stupid, stupid hope.

"How much more do you need for your feature?" he asks quietly.

In all honesty, I could probably get away with everything he's told me tonight. Between personal quotes and regurgitated stats from other publications, I've got enough on hand that Josh won't have any complaints. Still, I'm tempted to lie . . . tempted to tell him that I need so much more.

Seven days' worth of material.

But his rejection still stings, and the thought of wearing my embarrassment like a cloak for the next week deters me from fibbing. "I have enough now," I tell him, praying that I do. "Look at that, Mr. Harrison—you're already off the hook after only two days."

His brows come together like he doesn't believe me. "Are you sure?"

No. "Yep, completely, one-hundred percent positive. Now, maybe you can back off of me?"

He stays where he is, pressing his hard body against mine for a long, excruciating moment before peeling away. "This isn't how I planned for this game to go," he tells me softly, and I believe it. Duke Harrison may be a man of few words, but the open expression on his face speaks of regret.

Regret over nearly kissing me. Just what every woman wants to read in an attractive man's expression.

Ugh.

"It's fine," I say, yanking my coat back into place. "No worries. Thanks for—" I break off, waving my hand at the dartboard.

"Do you need a ride home?" he asks.

"I have my car."

"Right."

"It was nice meeting you, Duke. Good luck with the rest of the season."

I don't wait for him to tell me anything else. I hastily grab my bag from the couch, hook the strap over my shoulder, and hightail it out of The Box. No one stops me, and though I wish Duke would follow and ask me to stay, I don't hold my breath.

We've only met a handful of times. He probably feels awkward turning me down. He may not want Gwen, but he certainly doesn't want me.

I don't mix business with pleasure.

Yeah, I read that memo loud and clear. And I have no intention of seeking either pleasure or business with Duke Harrison again.

CHAPTER TEN

"*W*hat do you mean, 'it's lackluster'?" I demand on Monday afternoon, four days after my shit-tastic dart game with Duke.

Josh makes a show of perusing the printed copy of my article, flipping through the pages way too dramatically for my tastes. He tosses the stapled stack onto my desk. "It's no good, Denton."

My hands fly to the pages. Red ink mars the entire copy. "Can you tell me *why* it's no good?"

Josh readjusts his Red Sox baseball hat. "It's got no pizazz. No life. I could have been reading about root canals I was so enthralled."

What *is* it with this guy and the dentist? Whatever, it doesn't matter. I have bigger fish to fry. You know, like possibly losing my *job*.

"What sort of 'pizazz' are you looking for?" I throw in finger quotations because, what the heck. I'm four days away from being demoted to Josh's secretary-in-training anyway. Just the thought of having to sit in his office all day sends dread trickling down my spine.

I plow forward. "Not only did I speak to him personally, but I attended a game, on his dime. I spoke to his team-mates"—okay, *one* teammate whom I'd stalked all weekend on Twitter—"and I'm telling you, that article right there has more information on Duke Harrison than any other publication has put out since he last won the Stanley Cup three years ago."

Josh doesn't bother correcting me on any of that. He simply flicks up the brim of his hat, drags his coffee mug off my desk, and slurps the liquid down. Gross.

"It's bland, Denton. B-l-a-n-d."

"I know how to spell," I mutter, wishing I could slam my office door in his face. With my luck, the damn thing would probably fall off the frame. "I took up Hooked on Phonics at least fifteen years ago."

He doesn't laugh at my feeble attempt at humor. "You spent two-thousand words praising him in that article, Char-lie. Two-thousand." Pointing at the discarded papers on my desk, he adds, "That's two-thousand words too much for a player whose good days on the ice are solidly behind him."

I don't like where this is going. Softly, I ask, "What are you saying?"

"I'm saying that *The Cambridge Tribune* needs ratings, Denton. We need to spark a fire, cause a stir. We're being left in the goddamn dust right now and I can't let that happen."

Yeah, I *really* don't like where this is going. Not to mention the fact that *The Tribune* has always been in the dust. This isn't anything new. There are no phoenixes waiting for a cyclical rebirth from the ashes at this company.

Fisting my hands against my thighs, I mutter, "You want me to turn this article into a tabloid spread."

Josh jerks his head in a barely-there nod. "I want you to turn that article into something that's gonna catch fire and put *The Tribune* on the map."

Whatever I feel for Duke has no play in this. He doesn't deserve to be treated like paparazzi fodder. Sure, I may have felt slightly different about the situation a week ago, but even then I hadn't planned to trash the guy in the news. My intention hadn't been to slam him, but to shed light on a player's long-term career in the NHL. There's always a downturn, it's just a matter of when.

Swallowing past the lump in my throat, I clasp my hands together tightly in my lap. "I'm not comfortable with that, Josh. He's not a bad guy—"

The coffee mug slams down on my desk, liquid splashing over the rim as Josh literally explodes. "It's not about what you're *comfortable* with, Denton. I'm going to let you in on a little secret. We are five months away from shutting our doors."

Five months away from not having a job. A million and one thoughts filter through my head, all of them related to my meager savings account. "Maybe we can find a way to increase subscription volume," I throw out, opting for the positive approach. "Kick off a social media campaign. Get on Instagram."

"It's way too late for Instagram." Josh is pacing now, his feet thudding heavily across the carpet as he sharply cuts around and renews his path to the door and back. "We need something big. You need to make this article something big. It needs to be something that'll be picked up by *The Huffington Post*, maybe *People*. Hell, if *The Daily Mail* sinks its claws into it, we'll be golden."

All from one article about a man who has never made headlines for anything other than his stick play? Sure, there's been the rare which-supermodel-is-he-dating-now crap, but the media has always been more focused on his stats.

Not on his personal life.

I feel a little nauseous at the thought of being the vehicle that tears everything down for him.

"Josh, I can't do this."

My boss stops mid-stride. He's got that edgy flare to him again, the one that emerges moments before he cuts loose and flies off the handle. "I'm pushing up your deadline from this Friday."

"You have my piece," I tell him, pointing at my desk. "Four days early, even."

"It needs to be rewritten. I'm telling you, Denton, this shit has got to be good."

I'm not sure he even knows what he's asking of me at this point. "What if I don't?" I burst out. "What if I won't rewrite it, and you're stuck with these two-thousand words?"

"You're fired."

He says the words so succinctly that my mouth drops open. All I can do is blink back at him. *Fired?* "I thought my punishment for failure to deliver the copy was demotion."

"I've changed the rules," he says, sounding a whole lot like Duke from the other night. Josh's short, squat body swaggers over to my desk and grabs for the article. I'm almost not surprised when he proceeds to tear the paper into shreds, letting the pieces fall into the garbage can.

Shrrripp.

There goes page number one.

Shrrrrippppp.

Page two.

By the time he's working on page three, anger seeps out of my ears like those on cartoons I used to watch as a kid.

"New deadline is Wednesday, Denton. If that article isn't on my desk by three p.m., you can pack your things. You'll have the weekend to apply to those jobs you like so much at the *Boston Globe*—if they'll take you."

With that, he turns on his heel and stalks from the room.

With him, I swear he takes every bit of oxygen. I'm having a hard time regulating my breathing, for one very good reason: I'm so screwed.

I don't want to do this to Duke, but what choice do I have? It's either my job or my integrity, and never before have I been so torn between the morally right and the morally wrong.

You're better than this.

I am better than this. But I'm also struggling to get by, and while Duke has millions of dollars at his disposal, I have a one-room studio and a Prius that took me three years to save up the funds to purchase.

"Jesus, you look like crap," Casey exclaims, waltzing into our shared office with bagged lunch for the both of us. "What the hell happened when I was gone? You look like someone stomped on your cat."

"I don't like cats," I point out weakly, nearly breaking into tears when she hands me a Dunkin' Donuts Styrofoam cup, as well as a bagel and a chocolate donut. I plan to eat the donut first, you know, for emotional support.

Casey takes a seat at her desk, swirling around so she can look at me. "Yeah, I know," she says, falling back into our regular rhythm, "otherwise we could be lesbian lovers and marry."

I don't have the energy to play the game.

Instead I stuff my face with the donut and plot my next move.

A move that, no matter how much I wished it wouldn't, includes the NHL's golden boy, Duke Harrison.

CHAPTER ELEVEN

"*S*top moving, Charlie."

I freeze under the onslaught of Jenny attacking my eyelids with a makeup brush. She swirls more eyeshadow onto my right lid, and I do my best not to blink. "Are you almost done?"

"Almost."

"How much longer?"

Jenny snorts, and suddenly I don't feel bad about the way my knee is digging into her stomach. I'm sitting on the edge of my bed, head tipped back as my best friend tries to . . . prettify me, I guess.

If such a word actually exists.

"All we need is some mascara, blush, and you're good."

Thank God. I'd texted her in a panic two hours ago because, lo and behold, I'm attending a charity event with Duke tonight.

I know. I can barely believe it myself. Pinch me, please.

After messaging him earlier with the SOS, "BOSS WANTS MORE INFO," he reluctantly agreed to meet me. Only catch? He's attending an event tonight, and thanks to my looming deadline, I had no choice but to agree to this shindig.

I'm pretending to be a whole lot more put out about these turn of events than I am. In reality, butterflies have broken free in my belly and I've smoothed my hands over my dress no less than three times since I put it on an hour ago.

Another gift from Jenny, bless her heart. While our frames are completely different, we do wear the same size, something I've never been so happy about until now.

"Okay, done."

She steps back, admiring her handiwork with a tilt of her chin. Her hair is pulled back in one of those sharp hair claws, and a few strands fall loose to frame her face. Jenny has always been the "pretty" one out of the two of us, while I've always been the athlete.

Eagerly, I straighten off the bed and head for my full-length mirror, which is precariously attached to the wall.

Wow.

I barely recognize myself. My dress—or, rather, Jenny's dress—is a deep, cobalt blue that swirls around my ankles in varying lengths. The neckline plunges down between my breasts, giving a tantalizing preview of what's to come if I mistakenly lean forward too far. As for my face . . . It's me, and yet it isn't. My freckles are hidden under layers of foundation, concealer, and bronzer. The eyeshadow, however, I love. It's smoky and dangerous, and makes me feel a lot more edgy than I do in my daily life. To complete the look, Jenny has painted my lips a vampy burgundy, which I thought would clash with the dress but doesn't at all.

"You like?" Jenny asks, coming up beside me to stare at my reflection. Her hand lifts to my head. "Your hair . . . "

With the time constraint, nothing could be done to tame my mane. That's okay. It's proof that the woman staring back in the mirror is indeed Charlie Denton, and not some blonde seductress out to steal my identity.

"Thank you," I whisper, my hand finding Jenny's. I squeeze, just once, and then let her go.

Jenny grins. "I feel like I'm your fairy godmother."

"Promise me you aren't going to disappear at midnight," I tease, mainly to distract myself from my nerves. Duke agreed to collect me for the night, so that I don't have to worry about parking and walking in my four-inch heels from the car to the Omni Parker House Hotel.

The Omni, mind you, is the most opulent hotel in Boston. We're talking gilded hallways, gilded furniture, dark wood paneling that's less 1970s and more Golden Age America, à la Jay Gatsby.

I fake a bow, watching in delight as the blue silk of my dress parts to reveal a flash of my stiletto's silver ankle band. For a girl who has never been one for dolling up, I can admit, to myself anyway, that I look good.

"What time is Duke coming to pick you up?" Jenny asks as she starts to retrieve her makeup from where it's scattered on the duvet on my bed. She dumps brushes and eyeshadow pallets into a dusty, unzipped bag.

"Seven, he said." I peek down at my phone, checking for the time. Six-fifty. Almost show time. "I shouldn't be nervous."

"Then why are you?"

Because I think I might like him.

I'm not fooling myself into thinking that it's love. I've known him for almost two weeks, and that's way too soon to even be considering *that* particular four-letter word. Lust, on the other hand, is completely probable. I want Duke's company, even if I shouldn't.

Since I'm not ready to admit any of that, I deflect from the truth. "It sucks that my job is literally resting on this."

"So, do what you need to do."

"What's that? Quit and then starve?" I mutter, checking my teeth in the mirror for lipstick stains. "Your husband is going to just love it when I show up on your doorstep looking for a couch to sleep on."

Laughing, Jenny shakes her head. "You're not coming anywhere near my couch."

"Your floor, then."

"Charlie."

I turn at the serious note in her voice, my thumb falling away from my front tooth. Aside from her wedding day, I've never seen Jenny look so serious. Her gaze is sharply focused, her hands wringing in front of her.

"What's wrong?" I whisper, immediately reaching for her. I'm not one for too much affection, but I've known Jenny for most of my life. Seeing her upset makes *me* upset. "Is it one of the kids? Are they sick?"

Jenny's voice warbles a bit when she says, "No, no, it's nothing like that."

"Is it Ty?" I ask, referencing her husband. "Did something happen?"

"No, it's—" She breaks off, dragging a hand over her face in what is clearly exasperation. "Listen, it has nothing to do with the kids or with Ty. It has to do with *you*."

Well, that's what every girl wants to hear.

She doesn't give me time to form a thought before she's verbally plowing forward, her hands moving through the air in animation. "You've moved through your entire life on the defensive, Charlie. Your wall is up, always, and it's built like a linebacker."

"That metaphor doesn't make any sense—"

"Don't be a journalist for a second, would you?" From the amused glint in her eye, I know she's not mad. Thankfully. I have no idea where she's going with this, but once Jenny embarks on a mission, there's not much to do in the way of stopping her.

So, I murmur, "I'll try. For you."

"Great." Her hands settle on her hips, and I wouldn't be surprised if she starts pointing at me in the next thirty seconds. "What I'm trying to say is—"

The sound of knuckles rapping on the door interrupts her speech. It's Duke. One glance down at my watch proves that he's all of two minutes late. Late according to Jenny's absurd punctuation rules, but perfectly fine for me. I've never been early a day in my life.

"I've got to go." Swiftly I gather my small purse from the kitchen counter and press it against my chest. When I face my best friend again, she's ready for me, positioned in front of the door so that if I want to leave, I'll have to cut through her first.

"Charlie." She says it so seriously, so mom-like, that I drop my purse to my side and motion with my free hand for her to just give it to me already. Whatever she's got to say, just air it out once and for all.

She expels a deep breath. "I just want you to enjoy the night. You like this guy. Forget that he's a professional athlete. Forget that you owe Josh anything. Just allow yourself to have fun."

While I want to blow her off, I see where she's getting at. Since Dad passed away, my life has been less about the "fun" and more about what needs to get done. Funeral arrangements, college graduations, not starving to death. I'm not entirely sure I even know how to have fun outside work.

As much as it unnerves me to even say so, I whisper, "I'll try my best."

She doesn't fall for the platitudes. "Don't just try, girl. Have *fun*. For once, let yourself be swept off your feet. You may enjoy it more than you would have ever thought."

I give her a smile that's both grateful and a little disbelieving. Because while I can certainly pretend that Duke Harrison is my Prince Charming, there's still the fact that I've wrangled him into spending time with me with this interview. He's on loan, if you will, and by Friday, Duke will just be a memory that I pull out to enjoy, just like every other good thing in my life.

CHAPTER TWELVE

*T*he last time I was at the Omni Parker Hotel, it was my senior prom and my date ditched me at the last moment to take a junior instead. The junior, by the way, had a penis.

I know, I was just as surprised as you are.

While Joe and Jason danced away the night on the glossy hardwood floor like some handsome couple straight off a Ralph Lauren catwalk, I spent my evening devouring appetizers like it truly was the last supper. I smiled when my friends trotted off to dance with their dates. I shoved another éclair into my mouth when Jason, my former date, stopped by to say "hello," and to apologize for standing me up. For the duration of prom (four hours and twenty-six minutes of pure hell), I alternated between eating and skirting the edges of the ballroom like a true wallflower. It's a tough job, you know.

It goes without saying that I fully expected this charity event with Duke to trudge down a similar path. Or somewhat of a similar path anyway. I don't think I have to worry about Duke making out with a guy at some point during the course of the evening. Then again, you never really know.

But Duke surprises me completely.

He sticks by my side when we gather our food from the buffet line, and merely chuckles at me when I sneak up for seconds during the heartfelt speech from the charity's president. Duke sticks beside me when someone I recognize from college spots me within the crowd, and even goes so far as to press a hand to my lower back.

Like I belong to him.

It's a little ridiculous how eagerly I lean in to his touch, even when it's nothing more than a casual brush of our fingers as we clink our champagne flutes together at our table later in the evening.

He leans back in his chair, and the soft light from a wall sconce casts the lower half of his face in shadow. Not that it matters any. Duke Harrison is as hot in a pair of jeans and a plain T-shirt as he is now in a sharp, black tux. I've always been preferential to men in uniforms—firefighters are my total catnip—but now I can see why women go nuts over guys in suits.

Particularly, Duke Harrison in a suit.

His dark blond hair is slicked back and his blue eyes glimmer like finely cut sapphires. The Omni is ostentatious by many standards, including mine, but Duke looks right at home. If anything, he looks just as at ease now as he did at The Box, which is honestly the equivalent of a dive bar.

The ridiculous urge to crawl into his lap settles over me and I slap it away like a pesky fly.

Not going to happen.

"Thank you for coming with me," he says, wrapping a strong hand around the stem of his champagne flute. I'm half-surprised that it doesn't snap in half within his grip.

I match his movements and reach for my own champagne, just so that I have something to occupy my hands. "I probably should be thanking you, since I'm the one who's been harassing you for almost two weeks now."

He does nothing but grin at that. Then, his gaze heats as he gives me a slow once over. "Did I tell you how much I like that dress?"

A blush warms my cheeks. "Not in those exact words."

"Blades' colors," he drawls, drumming his fingers on the bowl of the champagne flute. "Is it too presumptuous of me to think that you might be looking for forgiveness for the Detroit jersey episode?"

My eyes dart down to my dress. Blue silk. Silver shoes. I didn't even realize that I'd dressed in support of his hockey team. *Jenny*. Of course. I glance at his face. "Do I need forgiveness?"

"No."

"No?"

He shrugs. "If anything, I owe you an apology."

My heart squeezes, and I drink from my champagne to hide my nerves. "For what?"

"I wanted to kiss you the other night."

He says the words so matter-of-factly that it takes a solid twenty seconds for them to sink in. Another fifteen seconds for them to be adequately processed. I lift up a hand, palm facing out. "Hold on, I'm not sure I understand. You're apologizing for *wanting* to kiss me?"

In a move born out of awkwardness, he lifts a hand to the back of his neck, and shifts his gaze away to the couples dancing behind me. "This isn't coming out the way I'd intended it to."

"I agree. I'm confused."

"Can I start over?"

Our eyes meet, blue against blue. I think of Jenny's words,

urging me to live a little, to enjoy life. "Ask me to dance," I tell him instead. "I might say yes."

He doesn't even bother asking, not with words. In a corny gesture that's straight out of a rom-com movie, he scrapes back his chair and stands, then holds out his hand in silent offer.

God, he looks good. So good that I almost forget the reason that I'm here to begin with. Employment. Financial security. The ever-present fear of never succeeding in my career.

I shouldn't be playing these games with him. I should be questioning him. Pushing him for insider's information that will keep my butt on *The Tribune*'s payroll, for as long as the company's doors stay open for business.

But I don't say no. The thought of feeling his arms wrap around me as we sway to a sickeningly sweet slow number is too great of a temptation to resist. The last time I entered the Omni, I roamed the ballroom aimlessly, wishing that someone would ask me to dance. This time around, I've made the first move and I don't regret a single thing.

Duke rewards me with a blinding, masculine smile when I place my hand in his. Then, the next thing I know, we're swaying on the dancing floor. Like this was the plan for the evening all along. Like we're actually on a *date*.

The thought is headier than I'd like to admit. It's a thought I'd do well to remember doesn't translate to reality.

As Duke's hands settle on the small of my back, I hold no illusions that this night is anything more than a sequence of dances and small talk. I'm not stupid, nor am I blind to the fact that once Duke discovers my betrayal, we'll never speak again.

My heart squeezes at the thought, and I dig my nails into his broad shoulders. The scent of pine swirls around me, heady and intoxicating, and I succumb to the temptation of pressing my cheek against his hard chest.

"Did I get you?" His voice is a deep rumble against my face. "If I step on your toes, I apologize in advance. I'm a shit dancer."

"I heard that all athletes are great when it comes to dancing," I say, enjoying the way he squeezes my hand as we shift around another couple. "I thought it was ingrained in your DNA or whatever."

"It must have skipped me." The hand on my back skips up to my neck and then flutters back down, tracing the beads of my spine.

"What else aren't you good at?"

"More fodder for your article?" He says it like he's in on the joke, but the guilt and worry over the truth stiffens my back in an uncontrollable flinch. If he notices, he doesn't say anything.

So, I pretend that I have nothing to hide. "I'm just curious."

"Are we playing Twenty-One Questions again?"

I shake my head, my cheek brushing the lapel of his tuxedo. "We don't have darts."

"We don't need darts."

Propping my chin on his chest, I tip my head back to meet his gaze. The lights in the ballroom have dimmed. The president has taken his seat, and the only conversation I hear is the quiet murmuring of dancing couples over the thunderous pounding in my ears. "What are you thinking, then?"

Intense blue eyes dip to my mouth. "You don't want to know."

"Maybe I do."

My heart beats rapidly, and I'm so consumed by the way his hands have come to rest below my shoulder blades, tugging me closer to him, that I barely register the fact that there's been a song change to something upbeat and flirtatious.

We're moving no faster than a sloth climbing from tree limb to tree limb.

Which is to say, I don't even think we're lifting our feet off the ground anymore.

Plus, let's be honest: I'd climb Duke if I ever had the opportunity.

"Are you planning to use this new intel against me in your article?" Duke asks, bringing my focus back to the conversation at hand. And not, you know, how good he feels snuggled up against me as we sway back and forth.

The guilt sharpens, twisting just a little too deeply. "I wouldn't. Ask me your question."

"No darts?"

"I trust you to play fair."

I have no idea what game we're actually playing, or if we're even playing one anymore.

Duke leads me around another couple, and then another and another, until we're flirting with the perimeter of the dance floor. Victorian-replica wallpaper lines the walls, and every so often a gold sconce is featured with a real candle—because the Omni Parker House is nothing if not authentically historic. The tables have been moved out of the way to make room for more dancers, aside from a large one at the opposite end of the room, where the donation table sits like a beacon of goodwill.

Unfortunately, my wallet isn't big enough for more than a single check. I'm blaming Josh for that, seeing as how he's already on my shit list.

"Why did you flinch when we walked through the front doors?"

His question catches me by surprise, and I don't manage to restrain the second jerk of my shoulders. He notices this one, too, and rubs his hands up and down my back in comfort.

His touch both soothes and arouses me, damn him.

"My senior year prom was here," I tell him quickly, like I'm tearing off a bandage from a festering wound.

"Had a good time?"

"My date decided that he'd rather spend some quality time with his best friend, Joe. Naked, in the restroom."

"Ah."

"Yeah."

"So, you . . . Did what for the rest of the dance?"

"Ate food, mostly." Pretended that I'd meant to go stag to prom the entire time. As that thought slides into fruition, another one follows on its heels: was prom all that important in the first place? It felt that way years ago, when my back and the walls of this ballroom became best buddies, but now that I think about it . . . I wasn't all that interested in Jason. It was the sting of rejection that had hurt a lot more than a truly broken heart. "I hung out with my friends, those who weren't shackled up for the night, anyway. Nearly demolished the entire tray of éclairs."

"What color was your dress?"

I lift my brow, mouth pursing as I look up at his handsome face. Now *that* I remember—for weeks, I'd stalked the local boutiques, waiting for the right dress to land on a sale. While Jenny had picked out her dress months in advance—read: Miss Punctuality Herself—I'd handed over my saved cash the weekend before prom. The dress had been sparkly and beautiful and . . . "Red."

"Like the Red Wings jersey."

Groaning, I drop my forehead to his chest. "You aren't going to let me live that down, are you?"

"No. Your turn for a question."

"How kind of you."

Although I'm not looking at him, I can hear the grin in his voice when he says, "I try—sometimes. When I'm not too busy showing my dick." He lets that sink in for a moment, giving me time to recall our earlier conversation, and I give a snort of laughter. "Go ahead, ask me something. Whatever you want."

I don't even give myself time to think on it. "What's your biggest regret?"

"My biggest regret?"

"Yes."

I feel his intake of breath, just before his breath rustles my hair. "Not kissing you."

Now it's my turn to breathe deeply. He's killing me. I swear to God, Duke Harrison is the biggest tease on earth. He may have women running loops around him. He may have not one but *two* Stanley Cups under his belt. He may have been the model for a *Got Milk?* ad however many years ago.

But when it comes down to making a move with me, the NHL's most popular goalie is tip-toeing around the line separating business from pleasure.

"Duke?"

"Yes, Charlie?"

"Kiss me already."

He doesn't need to be told twice. His fingers intertwine with mine, and he drags me from the ballroom. It's been years since I've last been here and I don't know my elbow from my knee. I don't think Duke does either, but he's not deterred in the slightest.

His gaze lands on the elevator. "This way."

And off we go.

With a quiet *ping*, the elevator doors swing open and we cross the threshold. The floor dips under our combined weight, not that I'm worried about it. I'm too busy hastily unbuttoning Duke's tuxedo jacket so that I can slide my hands beneath the material.

"Floor," I gasp, reaching blindly for the illuminated buttons to my right.

Duke does it for me, smacking the top button with his index finger, which just so happens to be the rooftop level.

Then, his mouth crashes down on mine, and I am so gone. He tastes like sex, there's no better way to describe it. Or maybe it's that he tastes like seduction. His lips tease at mine like he's sipping champagne, plying them open with flicks of his tongue.

Who am I to tell him no?

I give in, surrendering, with my back pressed flush against the mirrored wall and one ankle tucked around his calf muscle, needy for more. I'm not even embarrassed about the way I moan his name and rub shamelessly against him.

It's been a while, okay?

"Jesus Christ, Charlie," he groans against my mouth, one large hand cupping my face to better the angle of the kiss. The kiss turns even hotter, if that's possible. It's a tangle of lips and teeth, of captured sighs and hotter than hell moans.

"What?" I gasp. My hands go to his butt, which is firm and lovely, and I *really* want my legs wrapped around his waist.

"*You.*"

It's the second time someone has pointed me out like that tonight, but Duke's harsh whisper speaks to something very different than how Jenny said my name earlier this evening. Jenny doesn't want to get me into bed.

Duke's voice, on the other hand, is raw. Hoarse. Like he wants something so badly but doesn't know whether it's good for him. Like he wants to tumble me onto a bed, to hell with the consequences.

"Ask me a question," I urge him, mainly to distract him

from having any second thoughts and leaving me desperate and wanting. "Whatever you want."

His blue eyes sear me when they flick to my face. "Are you wearing any panties?"

A burst of shocked laughter escapes me. "*That's* what you want to know?"

"Right now, yes." His hand caresses my hip, and I watch as his fingers tangle in the fabric. The seconds tick by, slow and measured, as he hikes the silk farther up my legs. "Will you tell me?"

"No."

He pauses. "No, you won't tell me, or no, you aren't wearing any underwear?"

Just then, the elevator door *pings* open, and I flash Duke a saucy smile. "Wouldn't you love to know?"

"I would," he tells me solemnly, "I definitely would."

I've never been an exhibitionist. Hell, I've only had sex in a bed—missionary style. But Duke and I have been going back and forth for days now, trading barbs, trading flirtatious comments, and so it's not much of a surprise that as soon as we exit the elevator, we're kissing again.

Right now, I don't feel like an Ice Queen. I don't feel "frigid." If anything, I feel molten under his touch, as though I am seconds away from coming undone. It's almost . . . freeing, like that moment when you get home after a long day at work and unclasp your bra. You can't help but sigh with relief, even as you want to stretch your body to release the pops of tension tightening your limbs.

That's how I feel right now. My hands are in his hair, scraping back the layers away from his rugged features. His hands are cupping my butt, fingers tightening just so when I nip at his bottom lip and draw out a curse from him.

At once, I want to sigh in contentment and also to link my limbs around his body and beg him to make me come.

The thought of having an orgasm restarts my brain. We're making out on a rooftop, though the bonus is that we are hidden away in an alcove-like protrusion of a wall. The city's glittering lights fade behind the breadth of his shoulders. The hem of my dress slides up the length of my thighs, as Duke efficiently draws it up, up, up.

More importantly: *Duke Harrison is about to have sex with me on a rooftop.*

Words leave me on a marathon-worthy pant: "I have a question."

"Okay. Go."

"Actually, it's not really that much of a question." My dress is hiked up around my waist, almost exposing my lady parts to the world—or, you know, to Duke Harrison. This is just as nerve-wracking, actually. Forcing myself to ignore the distraction of Duke between my legs, I say, "I want to have sex with you."

Cool air kisses my belly, and I realize Duke has the fabric of my dress bunched in his fists. "That's good."

"That's *good?* That's all you have to say?"

Much to my surprise, he shifts his grip and presses me against his . . . Well, *hello* there. "Are you happy to see me?" I ask, lifting my hips to cradle his.

His only answer is to capture my lips with his, stealing whatever thoughts I have left from my brain. My article for *The Tribune* is the very last thing on my mind. Us having sex on a rooftop in Boston's financial district steals to the forefront of everything else.

A masculine hand lands between my legs. With a groan, he rasps, "No underwear?"

"None. You could see the panty line under the dress."

"Thank God."

After that, there isn't much conversation. I don't notice the chill in the air, especially not when Duke flicks his thumb against my clit. I don't notice the awkward way I'm positioned against a brick wall, save for the fact that Duke has lifted my leg around his hip so that he can slide a finger inside me.

I hiss with pleasure, driving my forehead into his chest, dragging my nails down his still-clothed arms. I want more. I want to see his tattoo for myself. Hell, I want *everything*.

My hand falls to his pants, over his hard-on. It's long and thick, and though I've never really had a good sexual experience, I can't wait for this one with Duke.

Duke, who is still one of the hottest goalies in the NHL.

Duke, whose smile is shy but whose humor is dryly delivered and complete with sexual innuendos. At least, with me that's the case.

My fingers find the zipper of his pants. "Underwear?" I ask, torturing him when I pull down on the tab but stop halfway to the end zone.

"None," he chokes out, "you could see the boxer line under my pants."

Laughter escapes us both, dissipating only when he curls his finger just so, hitting *that* spot, and my hand lands on his cock, tugging at the rounded head.

"Jesus, Charlie," he rasps, sliding another finger within me, hitting that spot again and again and again. "*Jesus.*"

"Do you want more?" I say, daring to press a kiss to the thick column of his throat.

"Fuck, yes."

His fingers leave me, and he quickly scans the rooftop. No one is here. We might as well be the only ones at the hotel. "Are you sure about this?" he questions, his gaze landing on my face. "We don't have to—"

"I'm one-hundred percent positive."

Oh, am I. Charlie Denton, Ice Queen No Longer. More than that, I'm craving his touch, his kiss. The cold is already seeping back into my limbs, reminding me that it's winter-time in Boston and that I'm wearing a silk dress.

Doesn't matter.

I'll stock up on Nyquil tomorrow, if needed. I'll buy orange juice and drink it by the gallon. I'll—

My thoughts scatter as Duke settles his tuxedo jacket around my shoulders. The scent of pine hits me like an aphrodisiac, and I want to curl into the coat. I flick my gaze up to his face. "Is this your way of telling me we're done for the night?"

I wait, biting my lip, for him to tell me to gather my stuff as he sends me packing.

That's not what he does at all.

His hands go to the zipper I've already halfway undone, withdrawing his erection and drawing his fist up and down in one hard stroke. Oh Lord, I can't find my breath. Duke Harrison with his hand on his cock is the hottest visual I've ever seen. I have no idea what I've done to deserve this, but I'm not about to start complaining.

"Condom?" I whisper, and he nods once, pulling his wallet out from his back pocket and removing a packet from the cash slot.

Magnum.

As if Duke Harrison could be anything else than magnificent.

"I plan to taste all of you later," he tells me, rolling the latex down his impressive length. "I'll start here"—his finger goes to my clit, which is tingling with need—"and then I'll work my way up to here." His fingertip brushes my nipple through the silk, and he laughs hoarsely. "No bra?"

"Didn't want any bra lines showing."

His forehead drops to mine. "You're killing me, Charlie."

"Same here." I squirm against him, and he lifts me up, settling me on what's got to be a brick level intended for plants. It's winter. It's freezing. There are no plants. Except for me, and I'm ready to bloom.

No, I'm not sorry about that wicked cheesy line.

"Stop making me wait," I say, urging him on when I clamp my legs around his waist.

He abides by my demand, thrusting inside with one hard stroke that has me calling out his name. My hands dig into his shoulders. His forehead drops to the curve of my neck.

"Fuck, Charlie," he mutters, his lips staggering kisses over my exposed collarbone. "You feel so good."

So does he. I lose myself in the eroticism of the push and pull of his hips from my body. There are no words that adequately define how I feel—needed, desired. For the first time in my life, I feel wanted by a man.

I've never needed to feel *wanted*. Over the years, I've learned to love my independent streak, to enjoy the life of a woman on her own, though fate handed me those cards too early in my life.

But in this moment . . . I want it to last forever.

"Please," I whisper, begging for something that I don't yet know the name of, "please."

Another kiss, this one to my forehead. "Whatever you want, sweetheart. You can have whatever you want."

With three more sharply driven thrusts, he gives me more than I could have ever asked for.

He gives me an orgasm.

He gives me a second orgasm. (Who knew such a thing existed?)

He gives me the hope that maybe, just maybe, we can be more than just random sex on a hotel rooftop.

Maybe it can lead to love.

CHAPTER THIRTEEN

I spend all of two hours deliberating on my decision for *The Tribune*.

Two thousand words, to be more precise.

I know what Josh wants of me. I know what'll happen when I don't hand over the "goods," so to speak. But after writing out an article that meets his specifications, I realize that I just can't do it.

I can't turn in something that, in turn, guarantees Duke's fall from society's pedestal.

Whether anything comes of me and Duke is just a bonus, but I can't force myself to type two thousand words of pure tabloid fodder. I tried, I really did. Thing is, bullshit only gets you so far when you're creating a captivating story.

By the time I typed the last paragraph, I was ready to vomit from self-disgust.

So, yeah, that's not going to happen. If Josh decides to fire me for writing the article that *I* want to write, then I'll tackle that obstacle when I reach that particular crossroads.

"You're smiling like a woman obsessed," Casey tells me from her desk. "Stop gloating."

I scrub a hand over my mouth, but damn it, the smile won't go away. "I'm not gloating."

"You're gloating." She swings her chair around so that she can watch me. "Go ahead, tell me how good the sex was again."

My grin feels like it could splinter my face in two, I'm smiling so hard. "It was great."

"Your attention to detail is lackluster."

I point my ballpoint pen at her. "Says the woman who refuses to write anything longer than one thousand words."

"Not everything that's longer is better," Casey quips, pointing her pen at me like we're in a battle. "Haven't you heard the saying, 'The size doesn't matter as long as you know how to use it'?"

My mouth drops open. "One, I don't think that's exactly the correct phrasing. And, two, please tell me you didn't just quote a penis metaphor."

"Concise syntax is sexy. I'm telling you, Charlie, shorter is better."

Lifting my hand, I shake my head, as laughter breaks loose from my chest. I don't think I've ever felt this *happy* before. If I have, it's been years, probably close to the time before Dad was diagnosed.

"You're sick, Casey."

"You keep saying so, but no one else agrees with you."

"They're just too polite to tell you so."

Still laughing, I switch my focus from my coworker to my email server. Quickly I scan the last line of the new article I've written: "*I don't plan on leaving Boston until Boston kicks me out.*"

It's perfect. Brilliant.

Honestly, if I hadn't written the piece myself I'd be praising the journalist who had. With a little prayer sent up to the journalism gods, I click SEND and release my new feature on Duke into the wild.

Or, rather, to the office downstairs, which has Josh's name plastered on the door like the calling card of doom.

It's Wednesday, two-forty p.m., which means I'm just ahead of my deadline. Which is great, because I have plans. Plans that involve Duke, me, and two pairs of hockey skates. He's taking me ice-skating to, and I quote, "see what I'm made of." All day, my excitement has been radiating like a physical force field that just won't quit.

"Leaving already?" Casey asks, already knowing the answer.

I clock out on the computer, and with a dismissive sweep of my hand, flick my trashy article about Duke into the garbage bin. I'm better than that nonsense Josh was spewing about on Monday.

"I'm meeting Duke at the rink."

"Sexy."

"It's not meant to be."

But as I drive two towns over to the ice rink, so that I can meet Duke for a skating session, I have to agree with Casey. Everything about Duke is sexy, from his good looks to the way he moans my name when he's deep inside me.

Call me a nerd, but what I like most is the way he looks at me. The way he teases a smile onto my face, even when I least expect it.

Okay, let's face it: I'm besotted.

I fancy the guy.

This time around, I think the guy fancies me too.

And that's unfamiliar territory, to be honest.

By the time I reach the rink, I'm a bundle of nerves. Although I met up with Duke yesterday for a quick lunch, this is the first time we'll actually be hanging out at length after I, you know, spent most of the night at his house after the charity event.

What? So I like sex.

I like sex with *Duke*.

This is not a crime.

Though I wouldn't be opposed to him whipping out a pair of pink, furry handcuffs. Just saying.

The parking lot is empty, save for a standard Ford F-150 parked near the entrance to the rink. And Duke, well, he's leaning against it, with his ankles crossed and his hands shoved deep into the front pockets of his jeans. Aviator sunglasses rest on the bridge of his nose, lending him a bad boy appeal that I find intriguing.

At the sight of me climbing out of my Prius, his naturally sullen mouth breaks into a grin and he kicks away from his truck to saunter over to my car. "You made it," he says by way of greeting when he steps into my personal bubble and fills my senses with his familiar scent of pine.

I try not to inhale too deeply like a total weirdo.

Going for a flippant response, I pat his hard chest and murmur, "Why would I turn down the chance to whip your butt on the ice?"

His hands wrap around my elbows, pulling me close to him. "Honey, the only one whose butt is getting whipped today will be your own."

My chin lifts and I make a show of staring him down past the bridge of my nose. "You sound so sure of yourself, Mr. Harrison."

"Hard fact, Miss Denton." His hands skip up to the base of my neck, his thumbs rubbing in little circles that urge a moan from my lips. "Don't make me start listing off stats."

"We'll be here all day."

"Exactly."

Our gazes meet and, as if balancing on the same thread, we simultaneously lean in. Our lips touch in a soft caress, so much softer than the other night. But this kiss is no less potent. I wind my arms around his neck, hanging on, forcing him to drop his hands from my neck to my hips to hold me steady.

It's the sort of kiss I used to dream about growing up. Lazy and easy, as though we are in no rush to head inside the rink and face off on the ice. But then Duke shifts ever so slightly and everything changes.

His tongue touches my bottom lip, seeking—no, *demanding*—entry, and I give it to him. Parting my lips on a sigh that he devours with a husky groan. Running my hands down the length of the corded muscles of his back. Tasting a hint of mint on his tongue.

The sound of a car door slamming to our right interrupts the moment, and Duke pulls back slowly. His mouth is swollen from our kiss, and something about that delights me like nothing else ever has.

After a moment, he clears his throat and rasps, "Obviously, you're trying to wear me down."

"For what?"

The grin he gives me is all sin. "You're worried you'll have to play dirty to win today. Still up to your games, I see, Charlie."

"I'm all out of games," I inform him with a flick of my ponytail. "Meet me on the ice and you'll learn that first hand."

He tips his head back and laughs, the deep, throaty laugh of a man who knows exactly what he wants. I'm not sure that the answer will be me a month from now, or even a week from now, but he catches my hand in his and leads me to the rink's entrance.

For now, I'm content just with this.

The guy at the front desk immediately recognizes Duke, and his placid customer service facial expression morphs into hero-worship. It's a little sickening, the way that Duke causes men and women to forget their own names. But, then again, he also makes me forget that I shouldn't hop into bed with a man I've known for less than two weeks.

So, am I really any better than . . . I squint at the guy's nametag. Sam. Let's face it: Sam and I are two peas in a pod.

The only difference being that I know what it's like to see Duke come undone in orgasm.

It's a sight I want to see again, soon.

"Hey, my man," Sam gushes, a warm blush roasting his cheeks. "You ready for tomorrow's game against Toronto?"

Duke's smile slips a little. "As ready as I can be," he says in the same tone that I recall from our double date. The bland, *I'm-giving-nothing-away* tone that truly is impenetrable.

Is he still upset after his loss against the Red Wings?

Sam rattles away, oblivious to Duke's mood shift. "You're gonna obliterate them. Man, I wish I was gonna be at the game tomorrow. It's gonna be one for the books, a wicked good game." He pauses while lifting our skates to the counter, as well as two hockey sticks. "Any chance you have a ticket laying around like last time? That was cool of you."

Silently, Duke hooks his fingers under the laces. "I'll pay on the way out. That okay, Sam?"

"Oh, oh yeah." The kid waves his hand in the air. "Not a problem. Honestly, I wouldn't even charge you but you know how my uncle is. No one goes in for free, not even his own flesh and blood. I'm talking about myself on that one."

"I got it, Sam."

Duke glances down at me, a look of impatience glittering in his blue eyes. "You ready, Charlie?"

"Sure, sure, I'll be right there. Just have to use the restroom first."

He nods, and his gaze takes on the look of a man who

isn't all quite present in the here and now. "I'll wait for you by the vending machines over there."

"Okay."

I wait until he's out of earshot before pulling my wallet out of my purse and sliding my credit card across the counter. Duke may be a millionaire—hockey players of his caliber always are—but something about the way he shuts down while talking about his career calls for me to . . . to want to take care of him.

It's stupid, I know. The man is thirty-four, as he's told me plenty of times, and probably needs no one. But if paying for his skates can put a smile on his face, even ever so briefly, then it's worth it.

Sam's hero-worship act has died off now that Duke is no longer with us, and the impassive mask is back in place. "You paying for both pairs?" he mutters, taking my credit card and tapping away at the iPad with the corner of the card. "You a friend of his or something? I've never seen you here before."

It's on the tip of my tongue to tell him that I'm Duke's girlfriend, but that's not exactly true. For that reason alone, I merely shrug my shoulders. "Yeah, I'm just a friend."

The words don't feel right.

Sam hands over my card and the paper receipt. "Have fun," he says, already turning his attention to the TV above my head.

Well, isn't he a charmer.

I find Duke by the vending machines, as promised. We climb onto the first row of bleachers, settling in beside each other as we start unwinding the laces of our skates, with our sticks by our feet. There's no missing the unhappiness that now cloaks Duke like a finely worn jacket.

There's definitely something going on there.

The journalist in me itches to push for answers, but the woman in me, for once, realizes the benefits of sitting tight and allowing him to speak when he's ready. Wasn't that exactly how I was, when my mother left and when Dad passed away? Jenny was my sole confidante for years, and even that open communication didn't come easily.

As if reading my thoughts, he mutters, "Sometimes it's nice not to have people ask you for favors."

My gaze drops to my skates, and I try to hide my surprise at his admission. "Like people asking you for free tickets all the time?"

His knee bumps mine. "Among other things."

Is he referring to me? I glance over at his face, and decide that no, for once he isn't throwing jabs in my direction.

"You ready to go?" he finally says, after we're both laced and ready to hit the ice.

I fall back into our regular routine, hoping to cheer him up in the face of a little competition. "Ready to lose, Mr. Harrison?"

His hand slides down my back before cupping my butt. His palm is as big as one cheek, and he squeezes playfully. "No dirty tricks out there, Charlie Denton."

Lifting my stick, I point the stick's toe at him. "I make no promises."

Blue eyes narrow in warning. "Thought you were over playing games?"

I choose not to answer verbally. As it always has, the ice calls to me, and it's been so long since I've had the chance to play the game. I slip through the partition in the low-framing boards, sucking in a deep breath the moment that my blades hit the recently shaved ice.

God, it feels amazing.

For the first few minutes, Duke and I do nothing but skate casually around the rink. We're the only ones here, seeing as how it's late afternoon on a Wednesday. He moves like a predator, hips slung low, broad shoulders barely shifting as he lets his powerful legs do all of the hard work.

It's fascinating to watch him breeze around, considering that for most of his career he's been stationed in the net, a warrior bent on keeping the enemy out. It's easy to forget that at one point in his career, goaltending was not his main priority.

Every so often, his head turns my way. He's assessing my form. Checking out the strength in my ankles and my grip on my stick. He watches when I pull my shoulders down, darting straight for the net, swooshing my stick back and forth as though a rubber puck is actually being carried down the length of the rink.

"We going to play anytime soon?" he calls out, pulling out a puck from his sweatshirt pocket. He drops the biscuit on the ice, drawing my gaze down the length of his massive body. In his skates, he's nearly a head and a half taller than me.

I tilt my chin up to get a better look at him. "You just going to let me shoot on you?"

"Open net," he counters, flicking the puck off the ice with his stick in a show-off move. "Let's see what you're made of, Denton."

I like the sound of that, mainly because I'm perfectly capable of holding my own.

We face off at the blue line.

"Who's going to drop the puck?" My hands grip the butt end of the stick, and I force myself to loosen my hold. Rule Number Whatever in Hockey: Never clutch the shaft like you're choking it to death. A loose wrist is everything.

Duke motions for me to hold out my hand, and then he drops the puck in it. "I'll let you do the honors."

"How sweet." My fingers curl around the cool rubber. "Feeling chivalrous again?"

"It's bound to pass soon. Enjoy the moment while you can."

Sensing that his mood is back on the upswing, I chuckle and position myself at the ready. "You're not going to let me win, are you?"

His gaze catches mine. "No way, Denton. I plan to savor this victory until the end of my days."

We'll see about that. Without giving him time to adjust, I drop the puck, make a *bzzzing* sound with my tongue and teeth (no whistle, you know?) and hack away at the black rubber, sneaking it away from him.

I let out a little whoop as I skate toward his net, leveraging my weight forward to keep my momentum going. One of the reasons that I love this sport is because of the burn. The burn in my calves and the burn in my thighs as I push to gain more speed. The burn in my eyes as I zero in on the net, disregarding all other distractions. The burn in my lungs, when I—

The puck's gone.

I twist around abruptly, years of practice allowing me to turn gracefully on the thin blades without falling flat on my face. Duke's joyous laughter reaches my ears at the same second that I see him swing back and send the puck flying at the five-hole.

My net.

Meanwhile, I'm all the way down on the other end of the rink.

This is not okay.

I protest this out loud when he does a small victory lap around the net.

"That was dirty," I mutter when we meet at the blue line again. "Your days of chivalry are over."

He reaches out and cups my face sweetly, then kills the

moment when he quips, "I told you to enjoy the moment, honey."

I brush away his hand, now more focused on the match at hand than any sort of romantic canoodling. I'm not a good loser. Never have been and seriously doubt that I'll one day learn that particular skill.

My hands tighten around the butt end, and I bend my knees in preparation to push off against the ice. "Let's play."

And so we do.

The game isn't pretty, that's for sure.

We battle over ownership of the puck, our sticks jockeying for control. No matter the fact that Duke usually spends his time in the net, he's amazing on the ice. And he's way better than I am—not that I let him know this.

We exchange trash talk like true professionals, delivering commentary about anything under the sun. He disses my stick handling. I insult the way he's too scared to hip check me, in fear of taking on a woman.

He promptly thwacks the puck away, and I misjudge the distance I have to reach for it, and go down on my knees. My teeth clash together at the bruising contact.

When Duke offers me a gentlemanly hand up, I take advantage, yanking him down when he's least expecting it, and drive the puck down the ice for a victory goal while he's still down.

He promises me retribution.

I promise to take him out for dinner after he loses.

We meet at the boards, shoulders jostling, crude language falling from our lips as we swipe at the puck. We throw our hands up in the air, in celebration of scoring.

But then something happens—the trash talk becomes a little more sensual, a little more like foreplay. Our battle for the puck at the boards becomes a little more personal, Duke's muscular arm wrapping around my waist as he pulls me away, or his hard chest pressing into my back when I wiggle my butt against his crotch in an attempt to throw him off his game.

"You keep doing that, I'll be introducing you to a completely different type of stick," Duke says in a rough voice by my ear.

"Is it still considered an introduction if I'm already closely acquainted with your . . . stick?" I push my butt back against him again, and his free hand clamps down on my hip.

"It will be if I'm aiming to take you in a different position this time."

My breath hitches at the provocative image his words have evoked. "Which position is that?"

His low chuckle rustles my hair. "Let's just say that I like the view from behind."

Oh boy. My knees? They're wet noodles after hearing that.

The whole Ice Queen has never been further than the truth than it is right now—which is to say that I don't have a sheet of ice left in my body. Despite the regulated cool air in the rink, Duke's close proximity is firing me up.

I sharply inhale at the feel of his hand curling around to my front and flattening against my belly. "How about we call it quits on this game?" he murmurs, tugging me against him. "We'll pretend that you won."

My hand drapes over his. "I did win. Don't forget who scored last."

"I can't forget something that didn't happen."

Whatever he might have said next is interrupted by the sound of his phone ringing. He uses a hand against the board to propel him back, and I twist around, still feeling winded with lust. It's a strange sensation, and not one that I'm accustomed to, but as I watch Duke's brows furrow as he answers his phone, I decide that there's nothing more than I want than to date this man.

It's probably a far-fetched idea, seeing as how we live two completely different lives. Not to mention the fact that I'm probably getting the can tomorrow morning after Josh realizes that I didn't deliver on his dream of tabloid trash.

Still . . . I suck in a deep breath when Duke lifts his index finger and mouths "sorry" to me. He doesn't *seem* to be biding his time before dumping me and chasing after the next puck bunny.

I wave away his apology and busy myself with skating figure eights in our area of the rink.

"Hey Gwen," Duke says, his voice a deep grumble that does funny things to my girl parts. "What can I help you with?" The space between his brows puckers a little. "Am I sitting? Why, you planning on dumping the mother-load of bad news on me?"

Drawing my hockey stick to waist-level, I slow to a stop. My ears perk up at the troubled note in his voice. It's the journalist in me. Curiosity isn't just a threat to cats in my line of profession.

But I'm also worried, too. The idea of something bothering Duke bothers *me*, which is terrifying, to say the least.

Duke turns away, just enough so that all I see is his profile. "No, I haven't looked at *TMZ*. It's not my usual day-to-day reading—okay, fine, I'll pull it up right now on my phone. Hold on."

Pulling the phone away from his ear, he taps away at the screen and I can hear Gwen's shrill voice through the receiver. It's jumbled and totally unintelligible, but, yep, she's howling on about something. As badly as I want to make a quip about untwisting her panties, I resist.

And then Duke's head jerks up, his hard blue gaze landing on me.

The look he's giving me? It's not the annoyed exaspera-tion from our double date, nor is it the bewildered want from the night we met up at The Box. It's not even the flirta-tious lust that has widened his smile and darkened his gaze each time he's looked at me since we hooked up on the Omni's rooftop garden.

No. Right now, he looks . . . betrayed.

My heart begins to thump erratically in my chest, so loud that I barely hear him say, "Handle this however you see fit, Gwen," before he hangs up his cell phone.

"Is everything okay?" I ask slowly, wanting desperately to skate backward and away from him.

Thankfully, he seems to be on the same wavelength as I am. "We're not doing this here."

Not doing what *here?*

I watch as he skates angrily toward the partition in the boards, and I scurry to catch up with him. "Duke," I say, just as he drops to the bleachers and starts unlacing his skates, "What's wrong?"

"Outside," he grunts stiffly. "We'll do this outside."

In near silence, we remove our skates and pull on our street shoes. Nike sneakers for him and Converses for me. He snags both sets of skates and hooks the sticks over his shoulder. I'm dying to ask him what happened, but I keep quiet on our way to where Sam is sleeping at the counter.

Duke lifts a hand to thump on the wall, but I put a hand to his closed fist, stilling him. "If you're waking him up to pay, don't worry about it. I already covered us."

If anything, my words darken his expression even further.

I have no fucking idea what's going on.

I manage to keep a rein on my need to chatter until we make it to my Prius.

And then Duke, who is notoriously tight-lipped, comes unhinged.

CHAPTER FOURTEEN

*D*uke's hands fly into his hair, raking through the dark blond strands.

"What's wrong?" I ask, this time more forcefully. "What did Gwen say to you?"

It's difficult to tell if Duke's eyes are blue anymore. The pupils have enlarged and his irises appear almost completely black. "What did Gwen *say* to me?" he explodes. "How 'bout I show you exactly what she told me to look up."

I don't think I'm going to like this very much. Still, I nod jerkily, realizing that his question is more rhetorical than anything else. "If you want."

"If I want?" A burst of incredulous laughter leaves him. "This isn't about what I want, Charlie. No, this is all—" He cuts off, a closed fist pressing against his mouth as he bites down on his knuckle. "You've been playing me from the very first second that you DM'ed me on Twitter. Fuck me for thinking otherwise—oh, right, you did that already too."

Confusion laces with worry as I stare up at his handsome face. "I have no idea what you're talking about, Duke. Could you give me a little more information?"

"I'll give you all the information you need." He whips out his phone, angrily swipes at the screen, and thrusts the device in my face. "But, wait, I've already done that, too."

My eyes adjust to the screen's brightness.

And then my stomach drops, this time straight to hell.

Oh, my God.

The headline, printed in bold red, typical of *TMZ,* reads: *NHL's Golden Boy might not have squeaky-clean image after all? Local Boston newspaper claims that Duke Harrison has hooked up with personal PR Agent, Gwen James.*

My first thought at reading this goes something like: *Fuck me.*

The second, more rationale version, proceeds with: *How in the world did anyone discover this when I . . .*

Oh.

Oh, no.

Josh.

The discarded article that I quite literally dumped into the trashcan just this afternoon.

Which means that . . . My boss didn't print the finalized version I sent him. No one has read the version which paints an accurate portrait of the Duke Harrison, Hockey Player Extraordinaire, while still lending both light and shadows to the man behind the pads and the caged mask.

The version that not only speaks to my skills as a top-notch journalist, but also doesn't spread untruths about the guy in front of me.

I'm going to be sick.

I actually press my fist to my mouth to make sure bile doesn't inch its way up my throat for an impromptu visit.

"Nothing to say?" Duke clips out, shoving the cell phone into his jeans pocket with a look of disgust. "Or did you get it all out in this article?"

Weakly, I whisper, "It's not what it looks like."

The oldest line in the book, and yet I can think of nothing else to say.

"No?" Duke shakes his head. "You know what's the fucked up part about this, Charlie? It's not the goddamned article and the fact that you've dragged two people down with you in your quest for fame. No, it's the fact that even while I *knew* you only wanted me for information, I didn't give a damn and still went after you anyway."

My lips part on a shaky exhale. "I'm not sure that I understand."

"Are you serious?" Another shake of his head, like he honestly can't believe that I'm this naïve.

Newsflash: apparently I am because I have zero clue as to what he's talking about.

"Contrary to popular belief," he says in a low, frustrated tone, "I don't sleep with every woman that comes my way. Maybe I did when I was eighteen and a rookie, but as you've pointed out frequently enough, I'm old."

"You're not old, Duke."

"Don't even play that game." He waves away my protest with a slash of his hand. "You intrigued me. You *still* intrigue me, and I'm a fool for letting myself think that you weren't after something more when you approached me."

Up until this point, I've been a very quiet participant in this conversation. The initial shock threw me, and so did the realization that Josh had betrayed every sort of professional line that should never be crossed. But listening to Duke now . . . I jump into the confrontation, verbal fists up swinging.

I am, through a messed up twist of fate, at fault in this situation. Still doesn't give him a reason to call me a gold-digger, though.

I fly toward him, my index finger at the ready to jab at his wide chest. "Don't play that with me, Duke Harrison. Sure, I pursued you for the sake of an article. You *knew* that. But the article is not the reason that I agreed to get pizza with you, nor is it the reason why I let you make love to me on a hotel rooftop. Or—"

Duke's eyes narrow and I physically take a step back. I actually fear the fury heating their blue depths. When he speaks, his voice seethes. "We didn't 'make love,' Charlie. We fucked. It was gritty and hot, but make no mistake . . . I don't love you."

The words hurt more than they should, forming like little shards of ice to puncture my heart. I shouldn't have . . . My eyes slam shut. I know that it's too soon for love. I get all of that. But hearing the nature of our relationship translated into nothing but base crudity is a ragged burn I did not expect.

So, I lie and I lie thoroughly, desperate to protect my bleeding heart. "I don't love you either," I tell him, irrationally wanting to hurt him as much as he's carelessly hurt me. "I couldn't love a man who hates what he does, and yet pretends to the world that that's not the case."

Pure silence.

For a moment, Duke does nothing but stare at me. "Excuse me?" he finally bites out, sounding angrier than even seconds earlier.

I promptly stick my foot in my mouth by saying the *utterly* wrong thing at the *utterly* wrong time. "You want to get on my case about this article?" I demand, pointing at his jeans pocket where he's stashed his phone. "Fine, do that. But don't pretend for one second that you don't understand what I'm talking about. You hate hockey . . . don't you."

A tick pulses to life in his square jaw. "I have no idea what you're talking about."

I saunter toward him, warming up to the idea of having the tables turned away from me. "That's the real reason you've been slacking on the ice, and it has nothing to do with skill. You've been purposely doing poorly, in the hope that the Blades won't re-sign you at the end of this season."

"You're delusional."

"Am I?"

"Yes."

"I don't think so."

He scoffs harshly. "I wouldn't be a fuck-up like that on the ice, Charlie. Nice try at averting the original topic—namely, you betraying my trust by spilling out this secret to all of America."

As much as I want to beg his forgiveness, I can see it in his gaze that he has no plans of accepting an apology from me anytime soon. "You wouldn't believe me even if I told you the truth, which is that I didn't submit that article to *TMZ*. I wouldn't do that to you."

"But you'd do it to Gwen?" he prods. "For what? Jealousy's sake?"

"I'm not jealous. I have no interest in emulating Gwen."

"Really." He says it like he doesn't believe me one bit.

"Really," I tell him smoothly, thrusting away the insecurities that perhaps he wishes I was a little more like his ex-girlfriend. Straightening my shoulders, I add, "I was in it from the beginning for the story. But if you can't find it in yourself to believe me when I tell you that the article you're reading on *TMZ* was not meant to go live, then I don't think there's anything I can say to make this right."

"Just answer me this."

I incline my head, a subtle sign for him to continue. "Go right ahead."

"Say I believe you when you tell me that my relationship with Gwen wasn't supposed to hit mainstream media . . . Did you still write it, thinking at any point that it might be published by *The Tribune*?"

The lie catches in my throat. However much I want to

pretend that I never second-guessed my morals in the last few days, that wouldn't be accurate. And so, sealing my coffin with the largest iron nail that there ever was, I whisper only one word.

"Yes."

His expression shutters, as quickly as a candle being doused by wet fingers. "That's all I need to know."

"Duke, listen to me. I promise that I never intended for it to go anywhere." I reach out a hand, then let it fall back to my side when he sidesteps me. "The *TMZ* piece was never meant to see the light of day, never mind be published."

His pulls out his Aviator sunglasses and slips them on to his face, effectively shutting me out. "Have a nice life, Charlie."

I take one step toward him. "Duke—"

"No, Charlie. Find someone else to play your head games. I'm no longer interested."

And with that, he stalks off toward his truck.

Leaving me to wonder at the pain throbbing in my chest, and the worry that I may have done the unthinkable—I may have let myself get in too deeply with Duke Harrison.

CHAPTER FIFTEEN

"*I* quit."

Josh's jaw practically unhinges as he stares up at me from his desk the very next morning. "Excuse me?"

"You heard me." I place my printed resignation letter on his desk. "I quit."

"You can't just *quit*," he grunts, panic effusing his tone with a tremble he can't hide. For the first time, I realize that I hold an ace. *The Tribune* is already crumbling. My departure, however unimportant at another newspaper, would mean the death of this one. "If anything," Josh adds, "*I* should be the one firing *you*."

"Too late." I tap the sealed envelope on his desk that contains my three hundreds words to Freedom. "I've already resigned. Considering the circumstances, I don't believe that I owe you a two weeks grace period. You understand."

He lurches to his feet and thwacks his Sox hat on the desk. "You're fired, Denton."

I've been working for an idiot for the last three years. "Josh," I say slowly, in case he's been having a rough morning,

"You can't fire someone after they've already quit. That's not how this works."

"Your writing is shit, Charlie. You won't find a job anywhere else than at *The Tribune*."

Ah, manipulating tactics. How surprising.

Not.

"I'll find something," I tell him coolly, already picking up my bag from where I'd placed it on a grungy chair. I'll tell you this. I am so effing ready to be on my way out the door. Who knew that quitting would feel so liberating?

I get halfway to the door when Josh speaks again. "I got news this morning that *The Huffington Post* picked up your article on Harrison. *The Huffington Post,* Denton. This could be career changing for you. Harvey Levin from *TMZ* already reached out to tell me he wants more of the same sort of leads from us. You could turn this into a regular gig, picking up intel on the Blades, and contributing to *TMZ* under *The Tribune's* name. Think of the possibilities."

Except that my "in" with the Blades is no longer speaking to me. Unsurprisingly, Duke has ignored my Twitter DMs. (It's crazy that we have yet to exchange phone numbers, and at this point, we never will).

To Josh, I say, "I'm not interested in that sort of journalism."

"Harvey loved your article on Harrison."

My hands close into fists at my sides. "Yeah? Well, did you tell him that you stole that article and published it without my permission?"

"My office, my rules, Denton."

"Exactly the reason I'm quitting," I snap, twisting back again for the door. Good riddance. Over my shoulder I add, "Just be thankful that I'm not suing you, Josh. At this point, I'll just be happy if I never had to see your face again."

I leave Josh yelling at me from inside his office. I don't

stop for the douchebags in finance, who regularly enjoy calling me a lesbian, nor do I say anything to the a-hole in the tech department, who once asked me to sit on his lap and call him "Daddy."

Screw that.

The only person that I *do* stop for is Casey. Not that I know why, because it's not like I won't be texting her later on today to give her all the details. Regardless, I stop at the doorway of our office and knock on the 1970s wooden paneling. Her head jerks up at the sound, and immediately I hear her mouse clicking away rapidly.

"Stop checking your dating website," I tell her, the first smile I've felt all morning stretching across my face. "Josh keeps tabs."

"I wasn't," she says, a blush staining her cheeks.

"You were."

She swings her chair around to face me fully, the way she always does, and threads her hands together before resting them on her stomach. "Lunchtime? I want some of those little tacos from around the corner."

"I quit."

"*What?*"

I nod, a little more happily than I should be considering that I'm now unemployed. "I quit. Just now. I'm heading home but just wanted to tell you."

Casey looks a little star-struck, and confirms this when she whispers, "You're my hero. Go fly away now, my little butterfly. Get the hell out of here and then text me as soon as you get home, so that you can give me all the details."

Casey and I aren't big huggers, so I promise to do as she says exactly.

Except, I'm not going home—not quite yet. There's someone I need to pay a visit to before I curl up on my couch and let the reality of today sink in.

. . .

"WHY SHOULD *I* HELP YOU WHEN YOU'VE SMEARED MY NAME across national news? Actually, I should be suing you for defamation right now."

I'm at Gwen's fancy townhouse in Brighton, one town over from Cambridge. Thank God for Mel, who provided me with Gwen's address.

And what an address it is—while I've been living in a one-room hovel, Gwen James is living life to the fullest. Her townhouse sits next to a pretty park, boasts a pool and lounge area, and even has the sort of grand, circular stairwell that every girl dreams about when she's seven years old.

Like I said—living life to the fullest.

Meanwhile, I've hit rock bottom.

Life's fun like that sometimes.

"Like I told you," I tell her, "The *TMZ* piece was never meant to be published. I wrote it to appease my boss, but I couldn't go through with it. I threw the article away and wrote something completely different for the newspaper."

"Do I look like a whore in that one, too?"

I cringe because, yes, in the first rendition, I had taken some liberties in telling the sort of story required of me to keep my butt on *The Tribune*'s payroll. But that story doesn't reflect my morals, nor does it reflect the sort of journalism I want out of my career. I'm not in the market for cheap shots.

Pulling open my bag, I withdraw a copy of the story that I wanted to write and place it on the coffee table. I tap my finger on the printed headline. "This is what I sent to my boss for review. You're mentioned briefly, but only to highlight the way you've helped shape Duke's career over the last few years. Words that came straight from his mouth. There's no mention of you otherwise."

With a move originating from clear suspicion, Gwen

leans forward and pinches the stapled corner with two fingers. Lifting it to her face, her eyes quickly skim the front page.

"You included the tidbit about his family . . . about their phone calls during the games."

I don't allow myself to feel hurt by her shock. It's expected, considering that the only recent article about Duke to hit the Internet is one that tears him to shreds. Clearing my throat, I say, "My angle was to examine the mindset of a professional hockey player over the course of his career, especially one so beloved by his fans."

Gwen doesn't say anything for a minute, and it is the longest, most painful, sixty seconds of my life. She flips her red hair back over her shoulders, crosses and uncrosses her legs at the knees.

Finally, she sighs. "I've known you for years, Charlie. I don't think we've always seen eye-to-eye—I know jealousy is a problem for you—but I want to be honest."

More honest than her telling me that I'm a jealous, green-eyed witch? Oh, do tell.

Not.

Since I'm fully aware that my plan will bomb without her assistance, I plaster a smile on my face and do my best to make it look authentic. "I appreciate your honesty, Gwen."

Gwen nods demurely like I've passed some sort of weird test. Then, she taps her fingers on her bent knee. "I know you want to talk with Duke. However, I don't think he's interested in talking to you."

"I owe him an apology."

"Yes," Gwen says without preamble, "you do owe him an apology. Duke has worked incredibly hard over the years to ensure a clean resume off the ice."

"I understand."

"No," Gwen counters stiffly, as she watches me closely, "I

don't think you do. If you had, then you wouldn't have thrown something like this back in his face."

My hands turn a little sweaty at her words. "What do you mean, something like this?"

"A woman using him to achieve her own career?" Gwen shakes her head, glancing up at the ceiling like she's in need of heavenly assistance. "Charlie, do you not pay attention to the tabloids?"

It's ironic, considering that my very last article for *The Tribune* ultimately became tabloid fodder across the country. In my personal life, however, I don't pay attention to the magazine rags.

I tell Gwen just that, to which she sighs. Loudly. "I've told Mel that you have no taste whatsoever, and you've just proved me right. Again. I hope you know that."

"I do now."

"I'm not going to tell you everything, Charlie."

"Because you want to date him?"

Gwen blinks. "I have a boyfriend. Why would I want Duke?"

Now I'm just confused. "Just a few weeks ago you were hanging on his arm and talking about engagements."

More blinking. I'm beginning to wonder if she has a sty in her eye. "Darling," she coos abruptly, "I have no interest in Duke Harrison. Sometimes I get carried away with the flirting, but that's just who I am. Not all of us can be such an Ice Queen like you."

Ice Queen.

For years, hearing the nickname thrown back in my face had the ability to pull me down for days. Hearing it from Gwen right now, however, doesn't affect me whatsoever. Maybe because now I know that it's absolutely not true.

I return the blinking, waiting her out.

"All right, *fine*," she snaps, smacking my article onto the coffee table. Her tea saucer shimmies under the pressure, and the liquid sloshes over the rim. "I liked Duke—*liked*. But he hasn't returned those feelings in two years, if not longer. He's not one to mix business with pleasure for a very specific reason."

Gwen would make an awful journalist. She has no knack for storytelling. No knack at all. "You mentioned that . . . Anyway you might want to fill me in?"

With a little cat-like hiss, Gwen straightens from the settee and begins to pace. "The only reason I'm telling you this is so you can see that you stand no chance of ever winning back Duke."

The words are harsh. I swallow them, digest the hurt that comes along with the insult, and push forward. "I can respect that."

"It was right after he won his first Stanley Cup. He was twenty-four, living on top of the world. It was his night to keep the Cup. Do whatever he wanted with it. Most of the guys took it home to their family, drank out of it—that sort of thing. Duke planned to do the same, except that he'd recently started dating this woman. She was a few years older than him. Awful cuticles. We go to the same nail salon."

My eyes fall shut and I count to ten in my head for patience.

I hit seven when she continues.

"So, Duke's been seeing her. He decides that on his night with the Cup he wants to spend it with her. They do . . . Whatever it was they were doing. He goes to bed, drunk and naked, and wakes up the following morning to find that his girlfriend is gone, the Cup is missing, and there are pictures of him naked plastered all over the Internet."

Oh, my God.

Duke Harrison was catfished.

Okay, maybe not *catfished*, but he was screwed over. One-hundred percent. How did I not know about this?

My brain quickly sorts through the information. This happened ten years ago, which means that I would have been sixteen and . . . completely consumed with helping Dad with the cancer treatments. Keeping up with celebrity gossip had been dead last on my priority list, if it had been on the list at all.

But that still doesn't explain . . . "How in the world has that story disappeared from the Internet? And what the hell happened to the Cup?"

Gwen gives me a dirty look, like I've interrupted her story time. "Good PR agents, a number of lawyers, and more than a handful of lawsuits. Keep in mind that this was just at the beginning of social media hitting it big. It was a lot easier to shut things down when you only had to worry about contacting certain websites."

I silently concede that this makes sense. Today, no amount of lawsuits would stop the spread of naked Duke Harrison pictures from blasting across the Internet. One minute his photo would be popping up on *TMZ*, and in the next, that sucker would be arriving in Australia for all the Aussies to ogle.

"And the Cup?" I ask. "Where did they find it?"

"At a strip club in South Boston."

"Classy," I mutter.

That feeling of being ill returns. Raking my fingers through my kinky hair, I ask, "How do you know all of this?"

Gwen shrugs one delicate shoulder. "He told me."

Ah. And yet he didn't tell me. For some reason, that bothers me more than anything else. But in the same breath, can I blame him? While we've certainly gotten to know each other, it's not as though I've revealed my inner secrets.

I haven't revealed how strongly I feel about him.

I stand up, my mind made up. "I need to find Duke."

Gwen's gaze flicks to mine. "Hope you're ready to fail."

People change over the years, but Gwen will always be petty. "I need you to take that printed paper and approach whatever news outlet that you think will print it."

With a shake of her head, she says, "Still looking out for only yourself, I see."

"I made an amendment to the end," I tell her, flipping to the last page of my feature on Duke. "I like him, Gwen. I like him a lot. I can do this with your help or without, but I'd prefer to remind you of a time long ago when you cried on my shoulder all night after your boyfriend broke up with you. He'd been sleeping with a girl in BU's marching band, right?"

Her eyes narrow into slits, and I know I've caught her. She drops onto the settee dramatically. "You're manipulating me."

"No," I drawl smoothly, sliding the papers toward her again, "Not manipulation. It's called a power play."

CHAPTER SIXTEEN

*I*t takes two weeks for the plan to be set into motion.

Two weeks of pacing my studio apartment, gnawing on my nervousness.

Two weeks of sending out job applications to newspapers, and only getting nibbles in return.

Two weeks of pure, unadulterated silence from Duke.

But today is the day.

I've already run through my lines in my head, having practiced on Casey, Caleb, Mel, and Jenny more than once during the last fourteen days. At this point, they've done a better job of memorizing my apology to Duke than I have.

Not that I haven't tried. It's just my jitters. They're making me edgy.

"You owe me for the rest of your life for this."

I barely spare Gwen a glance because I'm suddenly not quite sure that I can do this. I'm in the conference room at her PR agency in the heart of Boston's financial district, seated at a wooden table that could easily house fifteen people but currently holds only me.

MARIA LUIS

Cue a vomiting sensation.

I don't know if I can do this.

"Gwen, I—"

She cuts me off with a raised hand. "No. No way are you bailing on me right now. Do you *know* how long it took me to convince the CEO that this was a good idea? Tricking one of our clients into a fake meeting so that his frumpy girl-friend can kiss and make up with him is not in my pay grade."

I ignore the "frumpy" comment, mainly because I look cute today. Jenny dressed me, as per usual. My fitted black skirt, off-the-shoulder blue silk top, and matching black stilettos screams *professional businesswoman*.

The exact look I was going for when I concocted today's plan of action.

"What time did you say he would be here?" My gaze flits to my wristwatch. Ten-twenty.

"Ten-thirty."

Ten minutes until show time. Holy baby Jesus, I need to sit down.

Except that I already *am* sitting down, which doesn't bode well for what's coming next.

"If you're going to puke, do it there," Gwen tells me, pointing at the small garbage can in the opposite corner of the room. "Otherwise, I'll be back soon. Try to sweat a little less—you're looking oily."

And with that, she leaves me to my own devices.

Sunlight streams in from the window, toasting my neck and back until I worry I might start smoking.

I pull my hair off the back of my neck, and fan my face with my free hand. I am so effing nervous I'm ready to combust with anxiety.

Realistically, I know that I'm taking a big leap of faith here. There's a very good chance that Duke's interest in me has already waned, and that everything I've planned will be for naught.

It's a risk I'm willing to take. Under an umbrella of complete honesty, I want to see what could become of Duke and I's relationship.

My ears perk at the sound of voices on the other side of the closed door. There's Gwen's high-pitched tenor and Duke's low timbre. As I struggle to regulate my breathing, I watch as the door slowly swings open like something out of a horror movie.

Cue an influx of creepy as hell zombies.

And clowns—can't forget about the clowns.

"We have a lot to discuss today," Gwen says, motioning for Duke to bypass her with a wave of her hand. Since I'm seated to the far right, out of sight of the doorway, he hasn't spotted me. My cover hasn't yet been blown. "Congratulations on the win last night, by the way. Excellent save."

"Thanks."

I wince. He sounds . . . hollow, chilly, if that's even possible.

"The *GQ* feature will go live tomorrow, as well. I'll send you over the URL as soon as the editor alerts me that the piece has been published."

"Are you sure we needed to meet today, if we're getting everything taken care before we've even sat down?"

There's a small pause as Gwen positions herself opposite me, so that Duke is forced to present me with his back. I send up a silent prayer to the gods for allowing Gwen to put aside her bitchiness for the time being and to help a girl out.

"Sorry, Duke, I know you've got a lot on your plate right now, but I've brought in someone I would like for you to talk to about an upcoming project."

My heart flops over in my chest. This is my moment. "Hello, Mr. Harrison."

His shoulders visibly flinch, and I swear he stops breathing. The air stills right along with him, and I wouldn't be surprised if the temperature hasn't dropped down into the negatives. When he does speak, his voice is tightly leashed. "I'm not doing this today."

Bless Gwen's heart—I'm not even kidding, this time.

To everyone's surprise, including my own, she tosses back her red hair, lifts a key into the air, and cackles. Okay, so it's a perfectly perfect Oprah Winfrey-show laugh. Doesn't matter. What *does* matter is the way she practically prances to the door and announces, "Too bad, Duke, I made a promise. Oh, by the way. This room? There is no security video."

And with that, she sashays out of the conference room and slams the door behind her. With an audible *click*, the door locks, leaving Duke and I completely alone.

I doubt he's as thrilled about these turn of events as I am.

His back is still facing me, but I see the way his shoulders bunch under the frame of his jacket as he shoves his hands into his pockets. "Still up to your dirty tricks, then, Charlie?"

As much as I want to offer a sarcastic retort to that statement, I bite my lip and clamber to my feet. My ankle wobbles a little, thanks to the fact that I'm not accustomed to wearing such high heels.

Cutting around the corner of the desk, I move toward Duke, stopping when I get within a few feet of him.

"I wanted to talk with you," I tell him, wishing that he would glance my way. When his gaze remains resolutely on the wall behind me, I blow out a breath. "I also wanted to apologize."

His throat works with a hard swallow. "Apology accepted."

"I don't think you mean that."

Shoulders stiffening, he slams a palm on the desk and finally turns to me. His eyes are an unholy hue of blue, almost stunning in their vibrancy. "I'm done playing games, Charlie. Especially with you."

"Okay, great." My hands go up, facing out in front of me. "I'm done playing games too."

Mutely he stares at me like he's wondering what the hell I'm doing still breathing in his presence.

Thank God Gwen thought ahead and locked us in here. I never thought I might love her to death, but here I am, considering naming my firstborn daughter after her.

I lick my lips. "I want to start by saying that I'm sorry." My hands fall to my sides, fingers awkwardly tapping my thighs sheathed in a form-fitting skirt. "I'm sorry for betraying your trust. I'm sorry that, initially, all I wanted from you was material for my job. I'm sorry that I saw your downs as an opportunity to elevate my career to a new high."

Though the dark expression on his face certainly hasn't eased, his hand on the desk is no longer balled into a fist. A good sign, I hope. Since he doesn't seem inclined to respond just yet, I lace my fingers together in front of me and force myself to continue, for better or for worse.

"I'm sorry that I didn't tell you what my boss wanted of me or that—"

His raspy voice cuts off my pre-rehearsed speech. "What did your boss want?"

"Celebrity gossip." My gaze flicks away before bouncing back to the man who, in the short span of a month, has caught my attention like no one else has—ever. "Gwen was right when she said that *The Tribune* is one flush away from the sewer line. Josh, my boss, decided that the only way to keep the newspaper afloat was to revert to pushing gossip rags."

Retreating to the other side of the table, Duke folds his massive frame into a leather chair. He looks impenetrable, like uncut granite. When his hands settle on the table, his sleeves hike up, exposing thick wrists and tattoos on his left forearm.

A reminder that I haven't yet seen him fully naked. It's a travesty, I tell you.

Refusing to accept defeat in the face of his Cold War expression, I lift my chin and prepare to march to battle. "Josh gave me an ultimatum. Either I convinced you to give me the interview, or I was fired."

"I'm assuming you're living a cushy lifestyle now," he says in a low voice. The bright February sun has turned his hair to a burnished gold, though the hard planes of his face are cast in shadow. "*TMZ* pays a pretty penny for a salacious story."

"I quit, actually."

The line of his mouth tugs down. "Excuse me?"

Whelp, here goes nothing. "I quit. I admit full responsibility to writing that piece of trash that hit *TMZ* and then spread all over like a bad STD—"

"Is there such thing as a good STD?"

I ignore his sarcastic commentary. "I exposed information of yours that I shouldn't have. I did all of that." Moving to his side of the table, I push back the chair next to his and sit down gingerly, giving him time to adjust to my nearness. He doesn't move, which I take as a good sign.

"In my defense," I murmur, "That article was never meant to see the light of day. I wrote it, hating myself as I typed out the words. I'm not hiding from the fact that I'm ambitious or that I want to succeed, and I know that you joke about me playing dirty. But I promise you that I never gave that article to my boss. I trashed it, literally, and sent Josh something completely different."

"How different?" His voice is like the crack of a whip in the otherwise quiet conference room.

"There's no mention of Gwen in any other capacity than as your PR agent," I tell him honestly, hoping that he'll find it in himself to believe me. "I don't bash your stats, nor do I link your personal life to the game. I focus on the sport. I focus on your influence on the game of hockey . . . It'd be easier if you just read it for yourself."

"Charlie, I'm not interested—"

Determined to prove to him just how wrong he is about me, I pull my phone from my purse. With a few quick taps, I'm logged onto the proper website. Perfect.

Sliding the phone toward him, I wait for the realization to hit him that . . .

"What the hell is this website?" he growls, staring at the screen like he's looking at an abomination come to life.

He's not wrong.

"A free website," I tell him, fighting the blush making its way to my cheeks. "Originally, I had forced Gwen to make a connection with *The Boston Globe*, so that the *real* article could make its sweep across the Internet. The article that I feel represents me, as a journalist."

Duke holds up my cell phone, waving it about in the air. "And this thing is . . .?"

This time there's no stopping the blush from warming my skin. I reach up and tug my hair away from neck again. Does this room not have AC? Seriously, I'm burning up right now.

Seeing no other recourse, I mutter, "I built it. It's a free site." I squirm in my chair under the weight of Duke's searching gaze. "I didn't want you to think that I was using the weird fame thing from a fake article to bolster the one you're holding in your hands now. *This* is the article I turned in to Josh. *This* is the article I'm proud of. Please, read it."

He sets the phone facedown on the desk, and I swear that my heart crumples at the sight.

Time to opt for Level 2 of the plan.

"Duke," I try again, effusing warmth into my voice, "I know that your past isn't . . . stellar, but I want you to give this another go." I pull my hands into my lap. "Don't lump me in with what happened with Sam."

I don't miss the jolt of his body. "What do you know of her?" he demands, leaping up from the chair. "Who told you anything about her?"

"Gwen mentioned it, but I—"

Large, masculine hands drag through his hair in frustration. "It wasn't any of her business to tell you about Sam."

Crap, crap, crap.

Wrong move.

I stand, too, mostly to even out our height as much as I can. "Gwen just wanted to help me understand."

"Understand *what?*" Duke's hands fly up into the air, and I fall back a step at his rare show of emotion. "To understand how wrong I was to place my trust in a woman I'd only just met?" He laughs, caustically, and it's a devastating sound that rips me apart. "That I shouldn't have expected anything more from her than a quick lay?"

A few steps in his direction doesn't help any. He's on the move, tracing a path along the floor-to-ceiling window that looks out on to the busy streets below. I can spot the John Hancock, Boston's tallest skyscraper, as well as the Prudential Tower, where my father worked for a number of years.

The world beyond that window feels so very far away.

I place my hand on his arm, startled to feel the muscles in his forearm twitch under my touch.

I have no idea what I mean to say, but I'm saved from having to figure it out. To my shock, Duke covers my hand with his and . . . breathes. His eyes fall shut, and his nostrils flare with the intake of air. Blue eyes blink open, as deep and as fathomless as Boston's harbor in the dead of summer.

"I almost made it to the Stanley Cup twice before actually pulling it off when I was twenty-four," he says softly, his fingers brushing back and forth against the ridges of my knuckles. "It was the first season I'd played goalie. My coach . . . I don't know. He was desperate during playoffs. Merger got injured, bad, and then the second string couldn't find his ass from his head most days. We're up against the Capitals one night, and Coach looks at me from across the ice. He points, tells me to gear up and get in the net."

"Just like that?"

He gives a short, precise nod. "Just like that. I'd played goalie in high school for my first two years, had done reasonably well. Sometimes, during practice, Coach put me in the net just for shits and giggles, to keep me on my toes. That night, I was half-frozen in fear; worried I'd let in every puck that came flying my way. I was a wreck."

"It was the year the Blades came on the map."

A small smile lights his features, like he's thinking back on that long ago day. "Yeah, it was. I busted my ass out there on the ice, breathing nothing but hockey. But then I met her."

Ugly, green envy darts through my veins. I've never been one for jealousy. It serves no purpose, but right now, as I sit in this conference room with Duke Harrison . . . I feel its sourness filter through me. I don't much like it. Life's a whole lot easier when you can focus on the straight and narrow.

I nevertheless open my mouth and say, "You met Sam."

Another short nod, accompanied by a squeeze of my hand. "Yeah. She wasn't so much as a distraction as she was an outlet, an avenue to expend my nervous energy after long practices and even longer games. But then I started to like her, and while I was thinking of moving in together and long-term relationships, she was . . . "

"Biding her time, waiting for the moment to strike."

I don't want to say the words, but I'd rather they be out in the open. And while I'd rather not throw myself into the crossfire, I have no choice if I want to bypass this hurdle. "I can see where you'd start to liken me to her, but you'd be dead wrong."

Slipping out of my hold, Duke scrubs a hand over his jawline, then digs his knuckles into his eye sockets. He looks tired, beyond exhausted. "Whether you intended to or not, Charlie, you sold me out. You can beat around it, but the fact of the matter is, at some point you *were* considering submission to *TMZ*."

"All right," I snap, suddenly annoyed that he refuses to give even an *inch*. "So, yes, I wrote that piece. I wrote all about your personal life, Duke. But, hello! How would that be possible when you've barely told me anything about yourself?"

His mouth parts on what's obviously going to be a scathing retort, so I cut him off before the damage to my heart is permanent. I approach him with a swagger to my walk, intent on showing him just how wrong he is. "You want to feel bad about yourself? That's fine. You go and do that. But don't think, for one second, that you're any better than I am. Sure, I might want to be respected at my job, but you don't even *want* your job."

"That's not true."

"Then why," I say quietly, "have you composed two emails regarding your retirement in the last year?"

"How do you know about that?" His voice is as chilly as Boston on a frigid, February morning.

It's called being a Class-A Stalker when I want to be. That's not what I say, though, because I have no intention of being labeled as a creeper. Every source I've used has been completely legal, I promise.

Duke's feet carry him forward, until with his body he's cornering me against the window. With a little jump of surprise, my back hits the glass. It's cold against my exposed shoulders and arms. Cold enough to make the girls—I'm talking about my nipples—stand to attention.

Something Duke notices, if the way his hot blue gaze dips down to my chest is any indication. He gives a little shake of his head, dropping his hands to either side of my head on the window behind me.

Boxing me in.

Tempting me to thrust my hips forward and cradle his hard length.

"Charlie," he warns in a deceptively soft voice, "how do you know about the retirement?"

I close my eyes and take a moment to appreciate the way his body is inadvertently pressing against mine.

"Charlie."

All right, fine. "I spoke with *The Boston Globe* editor last week, before I'd decided to create my own website."

"Sean."

I nod. "You've approached him in the past about spreading the news. I may have promised him a date with Gwen if he talked, although she apparently has a boyfriend now."

Almost incredulously, Duke's eyes narrow. "He gave in that easily?"

"You fail to realize how many people want Gwen. Women, men, random strangers; everyone wants a piece."

And here we are, full circle.

"I'm no longer interested in a piece of her," he murmurs, drawing my attention to his masculine lips. I recall it pressed against mine, drawing moans from my soul and orgasms from other, more scandalous parts of my body. "I'm interested in—"

He cuts off, and I glance up at his face. He looks, dare I say it, a little bit nervous.

I can't restrain myself anymore.

"I want to see where this goes," I tell him fervently. "I want to see what your naked skin looks like with your tattoo, outside of the darkness of your bedroom. I want to know what your voice sounds like mid-morning, after we've already had sex and ate brunch in bed."

He laughs and the sound is music to my ears. "You're such a writer," he says, his fingers slowly planting themselves in my chaotic hair. "Are you sure you don't plan on switching from journalism to writing romance novels?"

"I never say never." My hands take a leap of faith and land on his flat stomach. "Maybe you feel differently, but I've never been so interested in a guy before." Time to rush through this, and hope to God I'm still left standing with my dignity at the end. My mind's eye reads over the last few lines of my pre-rehearsed speech.

"My mom left when I was a kid. My dad, as you know, died when I was seventeen. For most of my life, I've been alone and I like it that way. It's safer." Drawing in a deep breath for fortitude, I continue, somewhat mollified to see that the glimmer of anger etching his features has receded. "But then you walked into my life, Duke, and it wasn't meant to be anything. We met at a bachelorette party, and I wasn't even a bridesmaid. You had what I wanted, yes, but you pushed me. You made me interested, and that's . . . never happened before."

His eyes crinkle at the corners, and I feel his hands fall to my waist. "Are you saying that you're in love with me, Charlie Denton?"

Maybe. I don't know. It's way too soon to admit anything like that, though, so I try and play it cool. "I like you, Mr. Harrison. And I'm hoping, despite my mess-ups, that you might like me back. Even if just a little."

"I don't mix pleasure with business," Duke startles me by saying. When I try to yank out of his grasp, embarrassment lining my every move, he holds me still. "I'm not finished yet, honey."

The word "honey" stops me dead in my tracks.

I glance up at his face.

"I don't mix pleasure with business," he reiterates. "I learned that the hard way, when I landed on every major Internet site, naked as the day I was born, for months. For years I've been going through the motions, hesitant to trust someone to get too close to my heart. You're right—I've been ready to quit hockey for years now."

"Then why haven't you?" I ask.

"I don't know, and that's the honest to God truth. I don't have an answer for you. Maybe it's just a habit I don't know how to break. Get up, head to practice, work out. Rinse and repeat. For over ten years, the life of a hockey player has been my normal. But it became a routine that no longer challenged me, or pushed me to be something greater. And then I met you."

My heart starts to thump erratically. I'm trying to squash my hope—I really, really am—but I'm having a dreadfully hard time doing so. Since I lack patience of any kind, I whisper, "And?"

Duke laughs, pulling on a strand of my kinky hair with one finger. "And, crazy as this sounds, I met you and I felt like I had finally come alive. When you messaged me on Twitter, I stared at my phone for hours waiting for your response. You were ballsy, and your confident, take-no-prisoners attitude had me hooked from the start. I wanted to play your games. I wanted to do anything that would put you in my direct line of path."

Screw patience. Seriously, I'm done with it.

I throw my arms around his neck, almost going so far as to link my leg around his leg. Duke doesn't seem perturbed. He lifts me off the ground, his big hands hoisting me up into his arms, and then plops me onto the conference table without prelude.

"I haven't forgotten our rooftop sexcapade," he tells me, his calloused fingers thumbing the line of my silk shirt. "Have you?"

I smile. "No way. It was the best sex I've ever had."

"Me too," he murmurs. "I forgive you for the article. On one condition."

"Anything."

Duke leans down, pressing his weight into my body, so that my hands land on the desk to keep me steady. "Tell me, are you wearing any underwear today?"

Laughing, I playfully slap him on the chest. "You're a dirty man."

"I've got to be, if I plan on keeping up with your dirty moves." Then, he drops forward and kisses me. It's a different kiss than the others. This one speaks to the future and to commitment . . . and to love, I hope.

As he hikes up the hem of my skirt, his fingers flirting with the sensitive skin of my inner thighs, I say, "The answer to your question is no. I'm not wearing any panties."

With a groan, he plants another kiss on my mouth. "Charlie Denton, you're a keeper."

And, as it turns out, I am.

EPILOGUE

DUKE

SEVERAL YEARS LATER

"*D*uke! Mr. Harrison! Can you tell us how it feels to win the Stanley Cup for a third time?"

It feels like the best sex I've ever had. I don't say that to the reporters who are thrusting their voice recorders into my face. At thirty-six, I'm not interested in giving them shit to talk about on their blogs or whatever the hell they publish on nowadays.

The days where most of the reporters belong to print newspapers are long gone. Hell, the only dude I'll ever answer to has his own vlog on YouTube. Once a week he talks about hockey, and the two other days he's doing makeup videos or something.

Nice guy, though. Avid hockey fan.

I like him.

It's to him that I turn to when the crowd seizes up and hollers at me. "Stuart," I say, pointing at him so everyone else knows to shut up, "What's your question for me?"

"The first time you won the Stanley Cup, you got wasted and ended up with photos of your noodle being shared all over the Internet"—Stuart ignores my hard glare—"the second time, you stayed home and probably bathed in it."

"Is that right?" another reporter calls out from the other side of the conference room. "Did you bathe in the Cup, Mr. Harrison?"

No one cares about my nude photos anymore. It's probably because I'm old. Or maybe it's just because, while that time of my life affected me for years, it's old dirt for everyone else.

"No," I tell the woman who asked me a question, "I actually ordered pizza and watched Bravo TV."

The room erupts into laughter.

Stuart doesn't. He jostles another journalist-turned-vlogger out of the way, and goes on. "This is the third time you're taking the Cup home, Mr. Harrison. What're your plans for the evening?"

My gaze seeks out the one woman who never fails to capture my attention, who, after a year and a half, has my heart more now than the day we exchanged wedding vows. She's standing with a *Boston Globe* press badge clipped to her chest, and a notebook clasped in one hand. Her blonde hair is a crazy mess about her head, just the way I like it, and the smile that pulls at her lips is the best thing I've seen all day.

I turn to Stuart, though my gaze never leaves Charlie's gorgeous face.

"I plan to take my wife home, lay her out before the Cup, and make love with her until the sun rises tomorrow morning."

The crowd gasps with delight.

I don't bother to wait any longer. I hop off the stage, favoring my right knee that's been hurting all season, and head straight for the woman who woke me up and set me free.

❧

"You can't do that."

I don't tell Charlie that I can do whatever I want. I show her with my hands and my mouth, pushing her full figure against the bed covers and settling between her legs. My hand lands on her belly, which grows larger by the day with our child.

Two years ago, I'd never thought that this would be my life.

My fingers trickle down to the hot place at the apex of her thighs. "I can do whatever I want," I say, enjoying the way her back arches under my touch when I thumb her clit. "You told me so on our wedding night."

Her laughter catches on a moan. "I'm pretty sure that I didn't," she says, thrusting her hips up against my hand. "I'm pretty sure that was Caleb."

Probably so. Her friends have become *our* friends, and Caleb was actually my best man at our wedding. But since I like the way I can make her laugh, even in bed, I continue our game. My thumb circles faster, eliciting pants from her lips, lips that I can't wait to feel wrapped around my cock later tonight.

"Want to make me happy, honey?"

"Right *now*?" Her blue eyes peer up at me, frustrated.

"Right now." I kiss her forehead. "I want to make love to you in front of the Cup."

Her legs hike up on the bed, knees bending sharply when I slide a finger into her. "I thought you were kidding?"

Her words leave on a gasp, and I grin.

"Definitely not kidding."

"Right now?"

"I've been waiting for this moment for a year, ever since you told me about this fantasy of yours."

"But it was *my* fantasy—it can wait. Oh, my God, yes, right there."

I fucking love the way she responds so quickly to my touch. I love the way she calls out my name in bed, and out of it. I love her openness, especially when she shares her dirty thoughts with me. "It's my fantasy now, too," I tell her.

"You can't be stealing fantasies." Her leg hooks around my back to ensure I don't leave. "That's a cheap move."

"I learned from the best."

"Who's that?" she whispers, throwing her hands up to my shoulders and latching on. Charlie has been that way since the first time we had sex up on the Omni Park House's rooftop—she wraps herself around me like a monkey until I've satiated her completely.

I kiss her mouth, worshipping her with everything that I have.

Screw it, I can't wait any longer.

She's won, like always. It's a win I'll gladly concede because it means more pleasure. I shuck my sweatpants, inch my wife further up the bed so that she's comfortable against the decorative pillows she loves so much, and enter her in one, hard stroke.

We moan at the same time.

I'll never get over this.

I'll never get over her.

Charlie Denton Harrison came into my life during a time when everything was black and white. There was no reason I should have given her the time of day, considering that I'd made a point to evade reporters and the media after the nude picture showdown.

But then she called me overrated.

Told her friends that I probably had no real teeth of my own.

Maybe I'm a fucked up in the head, but in the span of sixty seconds, she had me, hook, line, and sinker. I wanted her, both in my bed and in my life. That scared me shitless.

The thought that I could see myself falling for her scared me even more.

They say that love sometimes feels like you're being hit by a bag of bricks.

No. Love feels like you've been struck with multiple pucks flying at the five-hole, and you've got no gear on to protect yourself.

I wouldn't trade it for anything.

Charlie lets out a keening moan below me. She's close. So close I can feel her body milking me for everything that I'm worth. Eager to push her over the edge, my finger finds her clit. My thrusts pick up speed, turning erratic when my own orgasm sweeps over me, starting in my balls and fanning out from there.

Like in some cheesy romance novel, her orgasm kicks off my own. I never close my eyes during my release, preferring to watch Charlie come.

She's the most beautiful thing I've ever seen. The fact that she's carrying our child slows me down, reminding me to take care, to watch my pace, but then I'm gone. Flying over the ledge, calling out my wife's name.

I feel her hand dip down my back, skimming the ridges of my spine. "I love you," she whispers, pressing a kiss to my head.

I return the action, kissing her forehead, the way I've done every time after we've had sex since that very first time on the rooftop of the Omni Parker House Hotel. "I love you too, honey."

Her fingers thread through my hair. "I'm so proud of you, you know."

"Yeah?" I prop my chin on her shoulder and meet her gaze. I know she isn't talking about the sex, as great as it was.

"To come back after last year's loss in the playoffs . . . They're going to be talking about this season for years to come. Might find yourself with another wax figure at The Box."

I laugh, because it's slightly embarrassing to have a wax figure at all, no matter where it's located. "You only get one."

"You'll be the exception," she tells me with infinite confidence. "I just know it."

"Maybe they'll add one for journalists who kick butt."

Her nose crinkles. "Doubtful."

"You never know."

I brush back her hair and press a kiss to the soft skin of her neck. "I've got some information for you, by the way." Another kiss, this one on her cheek. "Top secret clearance type stuff." This time, I ply her lips open with mine, claiming them in the same way I plan to do for the rest of my life. "Want to know what it is?"

Her blue eyes flare with interest, and I know I've caught her. My wife has no skills in hiding her inquisitive nature. "You're going to let me print this?"

I nod. "I wanted you to be the first to know. I've already come up with a headline."

"Tell me," she urges, her heels slipping up my calves. I'm still firmly planted inside her, and the motion jerks my hips and we both lose concentration for a moment.

But I won't be distracted, not for this.

"*NHL Goalie Duke Harrison Steps Down from Professional Hockey After Last Stanley Cup Win. He Plans To Spend His Life With the Woman of His Dreams and His Little Girl, Who Has Not Been Born Yet.*"

Tears seep out of Charlie's eyes. Laughter, I think. Her chest bounces up and down like she's trying to contain her mirth. "Son," she corrects me. "We're having a son, I just know it."

"Really, woman?" I snake my hands around her wrists and hike her arms up above her head. "That's all you have to say?"

"No," she murmurs, lifting her hips up to meet mine. I grow hard inside her immediately, proving that age really has nothing to do with anything when you've got the woman of your dreams by your side. "I guess if this is your last season, we're *definitely* going to have to fulfill that fantasy by fucking next to the Cup."

I stare down at her face, absorbing every detail that I know as well as my own. "No fucking—making love. Nothing less for Mrs. Harrison."

The sound of her married name tilts her lips into a sexy grin. "Okay, then, Mr. Harrison. I expect to be fully ravished."

I answer her grin with one of my own. "One ravishing on the way."

And then I pick up my wife and place her beside the Cup, and proceed to ravish her the way only a husband can.

Thoroughly.

Turn the page for a sneak peek of Sin Bin, Book 2 in the Blades Hockey series....

PREVIEW OF SIN BIN

The Blades Hockey series is now complete! Keep reading for a sneak peek of Sin Bin, the second book in the series. She's the Queen of Bad Decisions, and Andre Beaumont, the enforcer for the Blades, well, he's her biggest mistake...

I AM THE QUEEN OF BAD DECISIONS.

Now, before you start thinking that I'm overly dramatic, let it be known that, boy, do I wish that was the case. But no —I have a problem that's otherwise known as "no self-control." See the following:

A) My freshmen year at the University of Michigan, when I drunkenly professed my love for my English teacher via email. The recipient of that email? My professor. Naturally. The next day, I found myself on a transfer list to another class.

B) My ex-boyfriend, Mark, who apparently had a bad habit of humping his next door neighbor whenever I worked overtime. Discovering them together on our anniversary was just the cliché icing on the cake, and so was the way I stealthily slashed his tires the following evening, à la Carrie Underwood.

C) Andre Beaumont. Sorry, but we're not even getting into this one. I'll only mention that because of my . . . indiscretion—big muscles and silky smiles that hint at bed sheets and panty-dropping sex are always my downfall—my life has been one downward spiral for the last three-hundred and forty-two days.

But all that changes today. Here. Right now.

I flash a bright smile at the CEO of Golden Lights Media. Golden Lights is Boston's premiere entertainment marketing empire, and hopefully my next place of work. *Believe it and you will achieve it.* That might as well be my tagline. "I can't say thank you enough for asking me in for a second interview, Mr. Collins."

"Zoe." Mr. Collins utters my name the way some might say "Satan," like he's worried he might catch my plague just by sitting opposite me.

My smile slips, just a little. *Think of the job, Zoe. Think. Of. The. Job.* "Yes, Mr. Collins?"

Heaving a big sigh, Walter Collins drops back in his seat to study me with stoic brown eyes. "Zoe. Miss Mackenzie."

This cannot be good.

I gird myself for the worst, flipping my folder up against my chest like a body shield. It's packed with my résumé, cover letter, and three letters of reference. It's also packed with my hopes, which are seconds away from shattering, if the CEO's expression is anything to go by.

"Listen, Miss Mackenzie," he says again, scrubbing a hand over his bearded jawline. "You've got the right qualifications for the position . . ."

I know what's coming. The urge to scream is overwhelming. I bite down on my lower lip and count to ten. *One . . . two . . . three . . .*

"But while I'd *love* to welcome you onto our public relations team, I've done a little research since our preliminary interview, and what I've found . . . . Well, I can't say that I'm all too impressed with your professional conduct."

I'm sure he's putting that mildly, just as I'm sure he practiced that exact line in the mirror this morning. His words have a pre-orchestrated feel to them, and he delivers them somberly, in the same tone that my former employer oh-so-graciously gave me the news that I was fired. You'd think someone had died the way that he'd—oh, wait, that was my career.

Slowly I meet Mr. Collins's gaze, and I make the decision that I have nothing to lose. Not my pride or my dignity, nor am I harboring any longstanding too-high expectations. I know what the score is, and I'm willing to play to this CEO's fiddle, as long as I come out with a job on the other side.

"Mr. Collins," I say carefully, "I understand your reservations. But I can promise you that what occurred a year ago won't be repeated." Nervously I tap my fingers against the folder, internally debating how to approach the situation. I straighten my shoulders. "After my . . . transgression last year, I've had quite a while to think over my faulty decisions."

Mr. Collins does not look impressed.

Panic enters my body. After almost a year of applying to jobs in my field, Golden Lights Media is my last hope. My last hurrah. I'm twenty-seven years old and living with my dad and step-mom. If my dad has it his way, I'll be working at his restaurant full-time like a good daughter, while also babysitting my half-sister on my off-days.

I love Tia, but even my love for my twelve-year-old half-sister can't make up for losing out on my dream —permanently.

Mr. Collins doesn't know it yet, but he's about to offer me this gig as the new Public Relations Coordinator for his firm.

I plant the folder down on the desk with the flat of my palm. "Let's do a trial run."

"Beg pardon?"

Bam. Stifling the abrupt pleasure of throwing the CEO off his game, I say, "A trial run. You want to hire me, but you're not sure if it's a good idea. I'm convinced that you won't regret it. As you told me in our first meeting, Mr. Collins, my résumé intrigues you. I've worked for all sorts of mainstream celebrities, including some of Detroit's biggest sports stars."

Brown eyes narrow on my face. "Including Andre Beaumont."

My knee-jerk reaction to hearing that name is to throw something. Maybe pound back a bottle of Jose Cuervo, because there is *nothing* I would like more than to forget the feeling of Beaumont between my legs, as he proves once and for all that multiple orgasms are a thing.

Or, rather, a thing that can happen with men.

(To be fair, my vibrator does a solid enough job on its own.)

But I digress.

I clear my throat, awkwardly reaching for a small glass of water and downing half for fortitude. "Yes," I murmur, "my former list of clients does include Mr. Beaumont."

Mr. Collins studies me, his brown eyes unblinking. "Let me make sure I'm understanding you correctly, Miss Mackenzie. You would like for me to give you a trial run." He scratches at his perfectly manicured beard. "Does this entail assigning you a client? Do I hold you to the same standard as the other publicists on my team?" He drops his elbows to the desk and leans forward. "Do I draw up a contract that reaffirms that you are not allowed to sleep with a client just to be certain that we're on the same page?"

My cheeks burn with embarrassment, and the words die on my tongue. *It was only one time.*

It just so happens that the "one time" was also caught on camera. Then shared across the Internet.

I promise you, until the day that your step-mom texts you to say that she never knew about the birthmark on your butt, you're not living life hard enough.

When silence steals my tongue, Mr. Collins turns to his computer. His fingers fly across the keys, tap, tap, tapping away with all the speed of a Tasmanian devil on speed. He clicks the mouse, another click, two more, and then he swings back around to face me.

"All right, Miss Mackenzie." He folds his arms across his chest and stares me down over the bridge of his nose. "I'll go along with your trial run."

My heart drops clear down to my feet. "You will?"

Way to sound confident, Zoe.

"Yes," Mr. Collins murmurs, "I will. I'll give you one month, as you suggested. And one client."

I'm not sure whether I ought to cry with relief or laugh at the fact that my desperate ploy is working. I do a little bit of both, and Mr. Collins gives me such a stern side-eye that my sobbing laughter dies an awkward death in my throat.

Straightening my shoulders again, I realize that I'm preening. *Down, girl, down.* I drop my shoulders—lift my chin instead. "Thank you, Mr. Collins. Thank you so much."

Finally, *finally*, I'm catching a break. The first professional break I've been given since the entire world found out that I slept with Andre Beaumont, NHL superstar. The former right wing for the Detroit Red Wings. King Sin Bin, as raving hockey fans like to call him, thanks to his lethal skill set on the ice—a skill set which regularly lands him in the penalty box.

Maybe, if I play my cards right, I'll shed the dreadful nickname the media gave me—Moaning Zoe.

Maybe, if I play my cards right, I can finally get my life back on track.

"I promise that you won't regret this," I say, reining in the urge to gush. "Whoever you assign to me will be perfect, and I guarantee that Golden Lights Media won't have seen a better PR Coordinator."

There's a knock on the closed office door. I don't turn around.

Everything that I want is at this desk. My hands itch to sign whatever contract my new boss might have stashed away in the drawers. My heart stampedes in my chest, over-joyed with the fact that after three-hundred and forty-two days, I finally have the chance to prove myself.

I'm not just the woman whose career took a hard tackle.

I'm not just the woman crashing on her parents' couch, and watching the *Disney Channel* every night with her sister.

I'm not just the woman who threw everything away for thirty minutes of hot sex with the sexiest hockey player in the NHL. A hockey player who had no interest in talking to the media on my behalf. No, the jerk quietly accepted his trade to the Boston Blades and never looked back.

"Miss Mackenzie," Mr. Collins says, recapturing my attention. "You're in luck. My assistant, Gwen James, just signed a new client, and we're pretty eager to get him settled in with an agent who will keep him in line and ensure that his public reputation remains scandal-free."

"Scandal-free is my middle name, sir."

Okay, slight exaggeration. But it *used* to be my middle name, you know, before the whole thing went down with Beaumont. And it might as well be my first name now, since I fled Michigan to Boston six months ago in a life do-over.

If Mr. Collins picks up the irony in my words, he doesn't mention it. "One month, Miss Mackenzie. We'll be coming back around to this in thirty days. But I'm telling you right now—if I hear one sliver of gossip about you, your so-called "trial run" will become null and void. Do you understand?"

Do I understand?

Hell to the yes, I do. "Absolutely. You can be confident that I'll be on my best behavior."

"Brilliant." He gives one short nod, then presses a buzzer on his desk.

The door swings open as I turn around, and a woman with voluminous red hair waltzes in with a spring to her step. "Walter, I've got our new client here."

Her wide-eyed gaze lands on me. Oh crap, I know that look. It's the one I get when people recognize me. And by that, I mean, they've seen the banana-shaped birthmark on my ass, as well as a quick glimpse of my face from the security camera video.

Kill me now, please.

"Miss Mackenzie," she says, coming over to shake my hand. "My name is Gwen. It's great to have you. Walter already let me know that you're on board. I . . . well, let me introduce you to our newest client."

I try not to let my hopes lift. Golden Lights Media is the top public relations company in Boston. From actresses to sports heroes to politicians, Golden Lights has backed anyone who's anyone in the Bay State.

My gaze flicks from Gwen to the empty doorway. Who have they paired me with? I'm hoping for someone awesome like Mark Wahlberg. Maybe Matt Damon. Hey, a girl can dream, right?

When a shadow fills the doorway, an acute sense of dread settles in my stomach. That shadow is familiar and that body even more so. I tilt my head, squinting against the afternoon glare from the sun for a better look.

Leather shoes slip against the marble flooring as the shadow enters Mr. Collins's office. Inch by inch, the body emerges as my sight readjusts. Dark jeans cling to muscular thighs, and a white T-shirt is halfheartedly tucked into the pants.

Something about this isn't right.

I shift in my chair, wishing that I could see his face. I so want to reach into my purse for my sunglasses. Unlike Gwen, who pranced right into the light like a beam of sunshine, this person hugs the darkness.

"Miss Mackenzie," Mr. Collins says, interrupting my thoughts, "might I introduce to you our newest client?"

And that's when The Day from Hell is replaced.

Because out from the shadows emerges Disastrous Mistake Numbers One through Infinity.

"Hello, Zoe."

Andre Beaumont, the Devil himself.

Oh, hell no.

Want to keep reading? Sin Bin is now available on Amazon in both ebook & paperback!

DEAR FABULOUS READER

Hello there!

I hope that you enjoyed your time with Duke, Charlie, and the rest of the gang. I'll be honest, when I first started crafting this book, *Power Play* was a different beast. Charlie existed. Duke wasn't a hockey player (the travesty!!). There were still sexy times, because, hello, obviously Charlie and her beau had crazy insta-attraction.

I think that's the only part of this book that has really remained the same.

With that said, thank you *so* much for giving *Power Play* a shot (hehe, pun intended), and more importantly, thank you for giving *me* a shot, too.

Writing is an interesting thing. I've published material on medieval prostitution in England and in Italy, prostitution in 19th century New Orleans (oh, God, this is becoming a trend), ghosts and hauntings across America...but, in my heart, romance is where it's at. Historical. Paranormal. Contemporary. If there's smooching and flirting and hot guys, I'm there. There's nothing better than writing that first kiss or that first realization of, "whoa, hold on here, is it *you* I've been looking for this whole time?"

Power Play is my debut novella-turned-pretty-much-novel, and I truly hope that you'll stick around for more books and more fun romances.

My hope is that this Dear Fabulous Reader space will become a diary of sorts from me to you, so that we can grow together with each book. Without you, my manuscripts would simply sit on my desktop unread.

Now, before we (read: I) get all sappy up in here, lemme just say: I hope I'll see you next time, Fabulous Reader.

Much love,

Maria

ALSO BY MARIA LUIS

NOLA HEART
Say You'll Be Mine
Take A Chance On Me
Dare You To Love Me
Tempt Me With Forever

BLADES HOCKEY
Power Play
Sin Bin
Hat Trick
Body Check

BLOOD DUET
Sworn
Defied

PUT A RING ON IT
Hold Me Today
Kiss Me Tonight
Love Me Tomorrow

FREEBIES (AVAILABLE AT WWW.MARIALUIS.ORG)
Breathless (a Love Serial, #1)
Undeniable (a Love Serial, #2)
The First Fix

ABOUT THE AUTHOR

Maria Luis is the author of sexy contemporary romances.

Historian by day and romance novelist by night, Maria lives in New Orleans, and loves bringing the city's cultural flair into her books. When Maria isn't frantically typing with coffee in hand, she can be found binging on reality TV, going on adventures with her other half and two pups, or plotting her next flirty romance.

Stalk Maria in the Wild at the following!
https://www.marialuis.org

Or come hang out with her in her Facebook Reader group:
https://www.facebook.com/groups/MariaLuisReaderGroup